sew zoey

STITCHES AND STONES

written by
Chloe Taylor

illustrated by
Nancy Zhang

Simon Spotlight

New York London Toronto Sydney New Delhi

SIMON SPOTLIGHT
An imprint of Simon & Schuster Children's Publishing Division
1230 Avenue of the Americas, New York, New York 10020
Copyright © 2013 by Simon & Schuster, Inc.
All rights reserved, including the right of reproduction in whole or in part in any form.
SIMON SPOTLIGHT and colophon are registered trademarks of Simon & Schuster, Inc.
Text by Sarah Darer Littman
Designed by Laura Roode
For information about special discounts for bulk purchases, please contact Simon & Schuster Special Sales at 1-866-506-1949 or business@simonandschuster.com.
Manufactured in the United States of America 0813 FFG
First Edition 10 9 8 7 6 5 4 3 2 1
ISBN 978-1-4424-9802-0 (pb)
ISBN 978-1-4424-9803-7 (hc)
ISBN 978-1-4424-9804-4 (eBook)
Library of Congress Catalog Card Number 2013943452

CHAPTER 1

Woo-Hoo for Spirit Week!

Spirit Week is coming up at Mapleton Prep, and I can't wait! Every day has a different dress-up theme, so as you can imagine, it's right up my alley. There's Hat Day, Twin Day, Backward Day, Decades Day, and School Colors Day, so I've been sewing up a storm, working on outfits for the week. On Friday there's going to be a Spirit Assembly with awards for the most creative costumes and—believe it or not—a karaoke competition. Cool, huh?

I made this tulle skirt to wear for Hat Day on Monday, but I'm still lacking the most important part of the outfit . . . the *hat*! Hopefully I'll be solving the problem later today. My friends and I are heading over to Priti's house to raid her family closets. Her parents are from England, and as her dad says, the English are "Mad Hatters." Once, her parents were invited to Ascot, which is where the English hold famous horse races, like we have for the Kentucky Derby. People wear the most *amazing* hats. I can't wait to see what surprises Priti's mom has in her closet. She said we could borrow them if we promised to be *very* careful to not get them dirty. I told her not to worry; I'll guard them with my life!

We also have to practice the song we're singing at the big karaoke competition: "Be Yourself" by Las Chicas. I love that song; I just can't stop playing it— which is starting to drive my dad and brother bonkers. Since I'm the only girl in the house, sometimes I feel the need to stake out some territory (even if it's just by playing ubergirly bubblegum pop songs on repeat)! Besides, I'm just getting into the spirit for Spirit Week!

"So do you all have the spirit?" Priti Holbrooke asked her friends Zoey Webber, Kate Mackey, and Libby Flynn as she opened the front door to let them into the house. She was wearing a huge hat that bore a remarkable resemblance to one of the fancy flowerpots Zoey's aunt Lulu bought for her decorating clients except it was upside down.

"Well . . . definitely not as much as you have," Zoey said. "Where did you get the flowerpot?"

Priti laughed. "It's Mom's. She wore it to my uncle's wedding. Believe it or not, it wasn't even the biggest hat there."

"They must have had to rent a bigger hall just to have enough room for the hats," Libby said.

"Doesn't it give you a headache?" Kate asked. "Or, like, make your neck hurt from having to hold it up?"

"No," Priti said. "But it's hard to see out from under it. And forget trying to kiss people. I think they made up air kisses because of hats like this."

She pretended to kiss Zoey on either cheek with two loud "Mwahs."

"Help me! I'm being *hat*tacked!" Zoey cried in mock panic.

"Wow, I want to see the rest of the hats," Libby exclaimed. "But . . . I'm hoping there are a few that are a little . . . um . . . smaller?"

"No worries," Priti said. "There are plenty to choose from, but if you change your mind this one might still be up for grabs! Come on, let's go hat hunting!"

The girls traipsed up to the Holbrooke's spare room, where there was a big closet the family used for storage. The closet doors had already been flung open, revealing stacks of hatboxes, as well as hats piled one on top of the other on shelves.

"Wow, Priti, your mom must have gone to a lot of weddings!" Zoey exclaimed.

"And horse races," Libby added. "Didn't you say she went to Ascot with the queen or something?"

"Not exactly *with* the queen—the same day as the queen. On Ladies Day, when everyone wears fancy hats," Priti explained. "It's different in England. It's a more . . . hatty place. That's just how it is."

"I wish people wore hats more here," Zoey said with a sigh. She lifted one of the hatboxes off the pile and opened it. Inside was a white fascinator, which was constructed to look exactly like a sprig of orchids. "I mean, look at this. It's . . . perfection!"

"Oooh!" Libby squealed. "Can I try that?"

Zoey had been hoping she could wear it, because it would look amazing with the tulle skirt she'd made, but she said "Sure" and handed it to Libby, who slid the combs carefully into her hair.

"What do you think?" Libby asked.

"You look amazing!" Kate exclaimed. "It really works on you."

Zoey had to agree. And there were still plenty of unopened hatboxes to choose from.

Priti opened another hatbox and pulled out a pink, woven straw cloche with a white silk ribbon held in place by a cluster of mother-of-pearl stars. "Kate, this is so you."

Kate didn't look quite so sure it was her, but

then again she wasn't nearly as fond of clothing as she was of sports. Her favorite outfit was a team sweatshirt and a pair of jeans. Zoey, Libby, and Priti had to constantly work on her to spread her fashion wings.

"It's really pretty, but . . ."

"Go on, try it on!" Libby urged her, the orchid on the fascinator bobbing with enthusiasm.

Kate reached for the hat and plopped it unceremoniously onto her head.

"Fashion heathen." Priti sighed, arranging the hat to proper effect, and pushing Kate's hair back from her face.

She leaned back to examine her handiwork. "Much better."

"What do you think, Zo?" Kate asked.

"Priti's right, Kate. It looks gorgeous on you."

"Definitely," Libby agreed. "I love the shape. It makes you like an international woman of mystery."

"Okay, okay, I'm sold," Kate said. "But it's going to look kind of weird with jeans."

"You can*not* wear jeans with that!" Zoey said. "No way, no how! I'll lend you my pink tiered skirt.

It'll be kind of a miniskirt on you, but you can wear white leggings underneath. Libby, you have white leggings you can lend her, right?"

"Yes," Libby said. "And I have a perfect white shirt to go with them."

"And Sashi's got a pink belt that will tie the whole outfit together!" Priti exclaimed.

"She won't mind me borrowing it?" Kate asked.

"What is the point of having older sisters if you can't borrow their clothes?" Priti said.

Sometimes Zoey wondered what it would be like to have an older sister, but having her best friends to borrow clothes from was just **as** good. And being able to design and make clothes for herself and her friends was even better.

"What about you and Zoey?" Libby wondered. "We need to get you two hatted up."

"Fear not! The Holbrooke Hattery is not exhausted yet," Priti said, reaching to the top of a pile of hatboxes. She brought down a length of sparkly material.

"Wow! That material is sparkletastic!" Zoey exclaimed.

"I know, right? I forgot all about it," Priti said. "My mom got it a few years ago at a tag sale, because she knows I like sparkly things. I think she was planning to use it to make me a Halloween costume, but that never happened."

"We have to do something with it," Zoey said, letting the shimmering sequined fabric trail through her fingers. "It's too wonderful to sit in a closet."

"Okay, but right now you have to find hats!" Libby reminded them, reaching for the nearest hatbox.

She took off the lid and pulled out a retrolooking pillbox hat made of embroidered satin and topped with a veil.

"I think I like this one almost as much as the fascinator," she said, taking off the fascinator and trying on the pillbox hat.

Seeing that Libby had taken it off, Zoey picked up the fascinator and tried it on.

"What do you think?" she asked her friends.

"It suits you, too!" Kate exclaimed. "And it would look really cute with the tulle skirt you posted on your blog."

Even though she loved the pillbox hat, too, Libby looked a little disappointed.

"How about we wear each hat for half the day, then switch at lunch?" Zoey suggested to Libby. "The pillbox hat will go well with my skirt too. I can start with that one!"

"That would be awesome! Thanks, Zo! I like them both so much, it's impossible to choose," Libby admitted.

"What do you think of this for me?" Priti asked. She was sporting a navy-blue hat with a wide, angled brim, decorated with huge cream-colored flowers.

"I definitely vote for that over the flowerpot hat," Zoey said. "We can actually see some of your face, not just your mouth."

"And you can kiss us—or anyone else who might be kissable," Libby said, blushing.

"As if!" Priti said. She still hadn't forgiven Felix Egerton for asking Kate to the Vice Versa dance after he'd already said yes to her. It all worked out fine in the end, because the girls went as a group—without dates—and had a great time.

"And the color suits you," Kate said.

"Okay, well, now that our hat choices are settled, we need to practice our karaoke song," Priti said.

"Um . . . I've been thinking. How about I cheer you on from the sidelines?" Kate suggested. "Singing is not really my thing."

"But it's the grande finale," Zoey protested.

"Yeah, Kate. Have you heard *me* sing?" Libby asked. "It's not pretty. But karaoke is just about having fun."

"I know but—it's a competition."

Maybe it was from years of playing sports, but Kate usually played to win.

"No buts!" Priti said. "Everyone has to be a part of it. We're not just friends—we're a *team*. Besides, I'm working on the most *amazing* dance routine."

"Wait, we have to dance, too?" Kate asked.

"You *like* dancing," Priti argued. "You had as much fun as any of us at the Vice Versa dance."

It was hard for Kate to argue with that. They all had a great time dancing together.

"Okay, I give in!" Kate said, holding up her hands in surrender.

"Don't feel bad. No one can ever hold up to Priti pressure for long," Zoey said, grinning.

The girls took the hats they'd selected into Priti's room.

"So, are we still okay with singing 'Be Yourself' by Las Chicas?" Priti asked.

"Yeah! I love that song!" Libby exclaimed, and started to sing the chorus.

"I like it too," Kate said.

"What's not to like?" Priti said, laughing. "So, I've been listening to it and have an idea for a routine. Here we go. . . ." Priti put her MP3 player into a speaker dock and pushed play.

As soon as the first notes came through the speaker, she said, "Come on, stand up, watch, and then do what I do!" She started to show them dance moves.

Zoey watched her friend's feet carefully and tried to imitate her. But she found herself distracted by the noise that suddenly came from downstairs. The sound of loud voices. Angry voices. The voices of Priti's parents, who seemed to be having an argument. A very loud, angry argument.

Zoey glanced at her friends to see if they'd noticed. Kate's brow was furrowed, but that could be because she was concentrating so hard on trying to imitate Priti. But Libby caught Zoey's eye and gave her a *What is going on down there?* look.

Priti obviously heard it because she danced over to the sound dock and turned up the volume—loud. The kind of volume that would have Zoey's dad shouting at her to turn it down before she made him and Marcus deaf. But the weird thing was, Priti just went on with the routine, as if nothing out of the ordinary were happening. Zoey wondered why Priti wasn't saying anything and what was going on with her friend's parents. She'd never heard them shout at each other like that before.

But no one would guess from Priti's smile that anything was wrong.

"Come on, you guys! Let's do it again," she said, as bubbly and energetic as ever.

They practiced the routine until Mrs. Mackey came to pick up Kate, Zoey, and Libby, and Zoey thought if she heard that song one more time, she might wake up in the middle of the night sleepdancing. Zoey noticed that on the way out of the Holbrooke house, Priti's parents were nowhere in sight.

"See you tomorrow," Priti called from the doorstep. She waved to them until they were out of view.

"I wonder what all that shouting was about," Libby said. "I felt really awkward."

"I know," Kate said. "And Priti was acting weird."

"What happened?" Mrs. Mackey asked.

Kate paused. "Well, Priti's parents were arguing about something. It was pretty loud, but Priti acted like nothing was wrong, so I didn't want to ask."

"Me neither," added Zoey. "I didn't know what to say."

"Maybe she was embarrassed or felt like it was private family business," Mrs. Mackey said.

Zoey could understand that. But the more she thought about it, the more she realized that despite Priti's upbeat attitude, she *had* been acting differently recently.

"Have you noticed that when we make plans, Priti's been trying to go to our houses instead of hers?" she asked Libby and Kate. "I mean, today we went to her house because of her mom's hat collection, but . . ."

"Now that I think about it, you're right," Libby agreed. "Remember a few weeks ago? We were supposed to go to her house, because her mom was making new recipes for her Indian food blog and we were asked to be taste testers, and then all of a sudden she wanted to go to your house instead?"

"Oh yeah. . . ." Kate nodded. "And we were going to sleep over last weekend, and then for some reason Priti wanted to do it at my house."

"I wonder if it has anything to do with the big fight we heard today," Zoey mused.

"The best way to support Priti is by not letting your imaginations run wild with things that *might* be happening and be there for her when she's ready to talk about whatever *is* going on," Mrs. Mackey advised, glancing at the girls in the rearview mirror.

Zoey was determined to be there with a listening ear whenever Priti decided she wanted to talk. But in the meantime she had an outfit to finalize for the first day of Spirit Week!

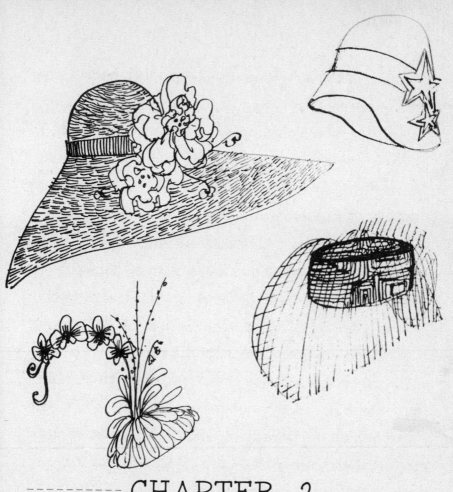

CHAPTER 2

Hang On to Your Hats!

Thanks to the British love of millinery—or the making of hats—my friends and I are starting off Spirit Week with the best outfits ever! You might be wondering why I'm not making hats myself. . . . Well, Priti's mom's hats were just too good to pass up.

Priti has a gorgeous navy-blue wide-brimmed hat made out of sinamay, which is a kind of straw, with a huge cream-colored flower decoration. She's going to wear it with a navy-blue skirt she's borrowing from her sister Sashi and a white chiffon top. Kate is wearing this totally adorable and perfectly pink cloche. The word "cloche" means "bell" in French, and it has a simple shape of a bell that looks great on her. We even managed to persuade her (well, by persuade I kind of mean ordered her) to not wear it with jeans. We cobbled together an outfit with Sashi and Tara's help (as in, they let Kate borrow some clothes). Priti is lucky to have not just one but two older sisters whose closets she can raid. Somehow I never feel the urge to go "shopping" in Marcus's closet! Wait—I totally wore his old shoes to school this year. Nevermind!

Libby and I fell in love with the same hats: An awesome fascinator that looks like an orchid and the cutest retro pillbox hat with a veil, so we are going to share. Libby and I were video chatting constantly last night, checking out different combinations of outfits to match. It's kind of like playing a clothing slot machine— mixing and matching shirts and skirts and shoes until the winning combination falls into place.

Ding, ding, ding!

And the winner is: still my tulle skirt, because luckily it goes well with everything. I had to try on fifteen different tops to figure out which one would work, and finally I settled on a pale green shirt that picks up the color of the orchid's stem but still looks good with the pillbox hat. Libby is going to wear a yellow skirt and a cream-colored shirt.

I can't wait to see what hats all the other kids are wearing. I wonder if our teachers will wear hats too? After all, it is Spirit Week!

I just hope I don't end up with hat hair. That's the only thing I don't like about hats. But everything else I *love!*

Mapleton Prep was a sea of hats when Kate and Zoey got off the bus on Monday morning.

"Look at Thomas! He's got one of those aviator hats with the goggles, like Amelia Earhart had. Cool!" Kate exclaimed.

"And what about Nicole! She's got a real

fireman's hat," Zoey said, pointing.

"You mean fire*woman*," Kate corrected, giggling.

"You're right, I do," Zoey said.

Much to Zoey's amazement, even Mr. Dunn, her social studies teacher, got in on the fun. He was wearing a multicolored beanie with a propeller on the top, and he announced to the class it was his geek hat.

"I'm a geek, and I'm proud of it," he said. "The geeks shall inherit the earth."

Zoey liked the sound of that. Go, geeks! She never thought Mr. Dunn would get into the spirit for Hat Day. Maybe he wasn't as tough as he seemed!

"And now put your books and notes away, because geeks should always be prepared for a pop quiz," Mr. Dunn said.

Zoey took it back. On second thought, maybe Mr. Dunn *was* as tough as he seemed!

Her English teacher was sporting a fedora, worn with an oversized jacket and slim dark jeans. Zoey loved everything about English class, except one of her least favorite people was in it—Ivy Wallace.

"Nice hat," Ivy said when Zoey passed by on her way to her desk.

Zoey was about to offer a surprised "thanks" when Ivy added, "Too bad you had to wear it with that outfit. What are you, six years old, wearing a tutu to school?"

It was hard to ignore Ivy's comments, but Zoey knew Ivy's goal was to see Zoey upset, so she just kept walking till she got to her seat.

"Wow, cool hat!" said her friend Gabe Monaco.

Zoey smiled. Ignoring Ivy just got easier. Gabe was wearing a shiny black top hat, like the guy on the lid of the Monopoly box. The hat sat on top of his brown curls, and Zoey secretly thought it looked kind of adorable on him.

"I love your hat too," she said. "It looks like it could be in a museum."

"It probably could be in a museum," Gabe admitted. "It was my great-grandfather's. Mom had it in a trunk up in the attic. She even had Grandpa's formal tuxedo."

"You should have worn it! It would have been awesome."

"I thought about it," Gabe said. "But I wasn't sure how into it people were going to get, and I didn't want to be *that guy* who came to school totally overdressed."

Zoey liked that Gabe was enthusiastic about getting dressed up for Spirit Week. When she looked over at Lorenzo Romy, her on-again, off-again crush, he had barely made any effort at all. Okay, he *was* wearing a hat, but it was just a regular old baseball cap, and he had it turned backward, just like he normally would. Nothing in the least bit special or spirited about it.

For today, at least, she figured that crush was off again.

All students were required to take off their hats for class, anyway, which was good because Gabe's top hat was kind of an obstruction to Zoey's field of vision. She was worried she might have hat hair, until she remembered today was Hat Hair Day as much as it was Hat Day. If she had hat hair, everyone would.

She talked to Kate and Priti in the hall on the way to gym. "Looking good!" she said.

"You too!" Priti said. "I just wish we didn't have to take off our hats for every class."

"Well, I have gym next," Zoey said. "I can't imagine playing basketball with a veil. I'm bad enough at scoring *without* something blocking my vision!"

Kate and Priti laughed.

"Just keep your eyes on the ball," Kate said, giving Zoey a hug. "And have fun. I wish I had gym now!"

"You wish you had gym all day!" Priti chuckled.

"Ha-ha. Good one, Priti! See you at lunch, guys," Zoey said. She didn't have the heart to tell Kate that gym was her *least* favorite class of the day. Zoey's father was a physical therapist for Eastern State University's athletics teams, so she kind of liked watching sports. She had to! But gym class was another story.

Zoey arrived at the locker room and placed the pillbox hat on a nearby bench while she changed into her gym clothes. She could hear Ivy and her friends Shannon Chang and Bree Sharpe in the next row of lockers. They were singing a song Zoey had heard everywhere lately called "Get Your Cool On." It was simple but catchy, and starting to grow on her.

"We're going to rock it on Friday!" Shannon said enthusiastically.

"You better," Ivy replied coldly, then added a halfhearted, "Just kidding!"

The song was okay but still not Zoey's favorite. *Well, it's perfect for them,* Zoey thought as she stuffed her backpack into her locker and hung her clothes on the hook inside. That's when Zoey felt a tap on her shoulder. She turned around.

"Hey," said Bree. "You forgot your hat."

Zoey was confused. "Um, thanks?" she said, watching in awe as Bree placed Zoey's hat in her locker for her. *That's weird,* Zoey thought. *Why is Bree being nice to me?*

Then the bell rang and it was time to go to the basketball court. Zoey tried to follow Kate's advice and just have fun, but it seemed like Ivy was making a lot of intentional fouls on her—and the teacher didn't see any of them. Another typical day in gym class . . .

When gym was over, Zoey changed back into

her regular clothes and headed to lunch. She was too hot and sweaty to put her hat back on. Zoey shuddered at the thought of having to return Mrs. Holbrooke's ladylike hat with post-gym sweat stains on it after she'd made the girls swear to keep the hats in perfect condition. Besides, she and Libby were going to switch hats at lunch in a few minutes, and Libby probably wouldn't appreciate a sweaty hat either. Yuck!

In the cafeteria, Zoey sat down next to Priti, set her hat down on the lunch table, and pulled out her lunch bag.

"What's for lunch?" Zoey asked Priti.

"*Saag paneer* calzone, I think," Priti answered, eyeing her lunch suspiciously. "My mom's been trying some hybrid recipes for her food blog, and I'm the guinea pig. Last night we had lamb burritos with naan instead of tortillas for dinner. "

"Lucky you!" Zoey said, then pointed at the calzone. "Wanna trade? I have a chicken sandwich with kale, peppers, and zucchini. My dad says it's fuel. For my brain. You know how he is. Actually, it's pretty yummy, but I love your mom's cooking."

"Yes, please!" Priti said, and the girls swapped lunches.

Zoey waved as she saw Libby approaching the table with her hot lunch tray.

"Hi, guys!" Libby said, sitting down next to Zoey and taking a bite of pizza. The orchids on her hat bobbed up and down as she chewed. "Isn't Hat Day so fun? How's your morning been?"

"Good," Zoey replied. "Can you believe even Mr. Dunn wore a propeller hat? He actually smiled today."

"Yeah, I know!" Libby said. "Too bad he had to ruin the fun with a pop quiz."

"Ugh." Priti groaned. "I have that later."

"Well, at least you'll have a new hat to cheer you up," Zoey said, handing her the pillbox hat.

Libby removed the fascinator from her own head and handed it to Zoey. "And here's the fascinator for you!"

Kate showed up just then, and they all compared notes on their mornings.

"I'm getting used to my hat," Kate said, opening the smiley-face lunch bag Zoey made for her when she got her braces off. "If it were easier to wear a ponytail with it on, I wouldn't mind wearing it every day."

"I can't wait to wear the fascinator," Zoey said. "Can one of you help me put it on, since I don't have a mirror?"

"I will!" Priti exclaimed. "But . . . aren't you going to have to take it off as soon as you get to class?"

"Yeah, but I want to take a picture for Aunt Lulu," Zoey said. "She would go gaga for this hat!"

Zoey's aunt was like a surrogate mother to her, ever since Zoey's own mother passed away when she was a baby. Aunt Lulu ran an interior design business out of her home. Over the summer, she taught Zoey to sew, and the rest was history.

Aunt Lulu had just left for Italy for a furniture design show, so she was missing the Hat Day spectacle. Her fourteen-year-old dog, Draper, was staying at a kennel while she was gone because Zoey's dad was too busy to take care of him. Zoey missed both of them terribly.

While Priti fussed with Zoey's hair and the fascinator until everything looked perfect, Zoey looked for signs that Priti might be ready to talk about her not-so-perfect situation at home. Priti seemed like her usual upbeat self.

"There you go!" Priti said, grabbing Zoey's phone. "Smile!" she added as she snapped a photo to show to Zoey's aunt.

"Thanks!" Zoey said. "How do I look?"

"Bee-yoo-tiful!" said Kate.

"Tall," said Libby, with a sly smile. "Almost as tall as me."

"I wish." Zoey sighed. "But it's not exactly easy to see over, is it? Kind of like Gabe's top hat. Did you see it?"

"He looked supercute in that, didn't he?" Libby observed.

"Yeah," Zoey agreed. "He did."

Her feelings about Gabe, Lorenzo, and the whole idea of boys and crushes were still pretty confusing, especially since the dance—when she thought dancing with Lorenzo would be the most romantic thing ever, but had actually had more fun dancing with Gabe. For now, it was easier to focus on creating cool designs than worrying too much about boy stuff.

When lunch ended, the girls all went their separate ways. Zoey was in science when the assistant principal, Mrs. Diaz, called her into the hallway and told her to report to Ms. Austen's office. She wasn't smiling, but Zoey shrugged it off. She figured maybe her blog friend and mentor, Fashionsista, had sent another parcel to her via Ms. Austen, as she had in the past.

Zoey stopped in the bathroom on the way to Ms. Austen's office, to put the fascinator back on properly. She loved that Mapleton's principal, Ms. Austen, had a great sense of style. Zoey wanted to make sure her special Spirit Week outfit looked just right.

Ms. Austen was waiting for Zoey outside her office. She was wearing a striped boatneck top and a beret with slim black capris and black flats.

"I love your outfit!" Zoey exclaimed. "It's *très français!*"

"*Merci*, Mademoiselle Zoey," Ms. Austen replied, but without her usual enthusiasm. She opened the door to her office and ushered Zoey inside. Zoey was getting the feeling that this wasn't about a package from Fashionsista or about something good. It was a feeling that was confirmed when she saw Libby sitting by Ms. Austen's desk, her hair streaked gray with some whitish powdery substance, and her eyes red and puffy from crying.

"Libby! What happened?" Zoey exclaimed. They'd only just recently parted from each other in the cafeteria after lunch.

"That's what I was hoping to find out," Ms. Austen said, sitting behind her desk, a grim expression on her face.

Zoey was confused. She'd do anything for Ms. Austen or Libby, but she didn't know what was going on.

"I put on the pillbox hat after you gave it to me at lunch and went to my next class," Libby explained, taking another tissue from the box on Ms. Austen's desk to dab at her damp eyes. "But then I had to take it off when class started and . . . well . . . saw *this*." She pointed to the mess on her hair and clothes. "Someone put what looks like baby powder in it, and it got all over my hair, my clothes, and the desk, which was bad enough, but then . . ."

Libby started tearing up again, and Zoey put her arm around her for comfort.

"But then people started laughing and pointing, and I started crying in front of the whole class." Libby sniffed. "That's the worst part of all."

Zoey understood how she felt. She'd hate to cry in front of Ivy. But she didn't think telling Libby that was going to make her feel any better.

"When Libby explained to her teacher that you and she had switched hats at lunch, Mrs. Brennan called me in to investigate," Ms. Austen explained. She leaned forward and looked Zoey straight in the eye. "I have to ask this, Zoey. Did you do this, thinking it might be a funny prank to play on Libby? After all, it's your hat."

Zoey's face expressed all the horror she felt that Ms. Austen would think she'd do something like that to one of her best friends, that she'd think upsetting Libby like this was funny in the tiniest way.

"No way!" she protested. "I would never . . ." Zoey turned to Libby. "You believe that, don't you?"

Libby nodded. "I never thought it was you. I told Mrs. Brennan, but she said it was 'just a little too convenient.'"

"For the record, I didn't think it was you either, but I needed to ask the question, just to be one hundred and ten percent sure," Ms. Austen said. She stood up and walked around the desk to sit perched on the end, next to Zoey.

"So what did happen?" Zoey asked.

"I looked up what class you have before lunch, Zoey, and I noticed Ivy, Bree, and Shannon are in that class with you. Did you put on the hat after gym?"

"No . . . I didn't," Zoey answered. "I was too hot and sweaty after playing basketball, and I didn't want to get it dirty, since it's Priti's mom's hat." Zoey paused, lowering her eyes. "I guess it's too late for that, now. What am I going to tell Mrs. Holbrooke?"

"Don't worry, sweetie. Baby powder will come out. She'll understand," Ms. Austen reassured. "But do you think it could have been the usual suspects? Could they have put baby powder in your hat during gym?"

Knowing Ivy and her crew, Zoey thought they might have had something to do with it, but it wasn't like she actually *saw* anyone doing anything, and she wasn't about to be a tattletale. So she just shrugged and said, "I don't know," then remembered that Bree had reminded her to put her hat in her locker. "Actually, Bree *was* kind of nice to me today."

Ms. Austen held her gaze for a moment and then stood up.

"Well, I think I might just ask them to come to my office and have a chat, just in case," she said.

As much as Zoey wanted Ivy to get in trouble if it *was* her behind the prank that upset Libby so much, she had a sinking feeling that somehow Ms. Austen having a chat with Ivy and her gang was just going to end up making things worse.

"I'll give you each a pass to go back to class," Ms. Austen said. "Zoey, perhaps you can accompany Libby to the restroom first and help her clean up."

"Sure," Zoey said, taking her pass and Libby's and picking up the powdery pillbox hat from the desk.

"I don't want to go back to class," Libby confessed to Zoey when they entered the nearest restroom. "I'm so embarrassed about what happened."

Zoey was busy wiping the remaining powder from the pillbox hat with a paper towel.

"*You* shouldn't be embarrassed," she said. "The person who did this is the one who should be."

Placing the hat carefully on the edge of the sink, she said, "How about I help you get the powder out of your hair?"

"Thanks." Libby sighed.

Zoey combed her fingers through Libby's hair, fluffing out the particles of powder.

"You know, I think that prank was aimed at me," she said. "Except I was too hot after gym, so I didn't put the hat back on before I gave it to you." She hugged Libby. "I'm really sorry it ended up being you."

Libby hugged her back. "It shouldn't have been either of us," she said. "It was a dumb thing to do."

"I know. I'm just sorry . . . you know . . ."

"I know," Libby said. "It's not your fault. Thanks for helping me get cleaned up."

"Well, it's not all gone, but it'll come out in the shower. At least you smell really nice!" Zoey said, getting Libby to crack a little smile.

They both headed back to class, neither one of them feeling too good about the situation. Zoey was too worried about the fallout from Ms. Austen talking to Ivy, Shannon, and Bree.

When she met Priti and Kate later that day, the school was already buzzing with rumors.

"I heard Ivy made Bree do it by threatening not to be her friend anymore if she didn't," Kate said.

"Well, apparently, Ms. Austen gave *all three of them* a very serious warning and said if she can find proof that they're responsible, or if they misbehave again, they'll be in big trouble," Priti said.

Although part of Zoey knew it was a good thing they'd received a serious warning from Ms. Austen, another part felt anxious, wondering if Ivy would end up retaliating. She felt like she would need to look over her shoulder for the rest of Hat Day.

Then Zoey ran into Libby in the hall. Libby looked upset again.

"Libby! Are you okay?" Zoey asked. "I thought you were feeling a little better."

"I got in trouble," she said. "I didn't want to take my hat off for class, because I was afraid people might laugh at my hair. So my teacher gave me a detention for tomorrow."

"But . . . that's not fair!" Zoey exclaimed. "I'm sure if you explain to Ms. Austen . . ."

"I'm on my way to see her now," Libby said. "I'm going to ask Mom to pick me up."

As she walked to her next class, Zoey's fists were clenched around her notebook. Hat Day started off being so much fun, and now Libby was upset and going home, all because someone was mean and played a stupid prank. It just wasn't fair. Zoey thought back to how ladylike and grown-up she and Libby had felt in their hats earlier that day . . . before Libby was the victim of that very unladylike prank. Maybe the whole thing was meant to be a joke. But seeing Libby that upset just wasn't funny.

Still, tomorrow was Twin Day. Zoey and her friends had worked hard on their costumes. It was bound to be a better day. It had to be.

-------- CHAPTER 3 --------

An Outfit to Tie-Dye for!

I haven't started off Spirit Week in such great spirits. Someone pulled a horrible hat prank today, putting powder in the pillbox hat when I left it in the locker room during gym. I have my suspicions about who did it, but since I don't have proof, I'm not saying anything.

But their prank went wrong. I was going to switch hats with Libby at lunch, and since I was hot after all that running around, playing basketball, I didn't put the hat back on. That's how poor Libby ended up being the one who got pranked. When she took off the hat in class after the switch, powder got everywhere—in her hair, on her clothes, on the desk. The whole thing was so upsetting, she ended up going home a little early. I wonder if the people who did it realize the stupid thing they did ended up ruining someone's entire day? If they do, does it make them feel even the teensiest bit bad?

At least tomorrow is a new day: TWIN DAY! I designed and helped make these outfits for all of us. The principal said Twin Day could mean anything from dressing in the same outfits to being dressed as perfect pairs, things that go well together.

So, of course, our first thought was to do something related to food. Kate and Libby decided to be a milk bottle and Oreo cookie. To save time, I made the costumes by altering the shape of plain dresses from the thrift store. Then I designed collars, trim, and an Oreo cream belt, and Kate and Libby helped put it all together. I asked Priti if she would want to be peanut butter and jelly, but she doesn't like PB&J. Apparently, her mom doesn't like peanut butter, so Priti never developed a taste for it. And Priti's dad grew up eating this stuff called Marmite in England. I tried Marmite once when I was over at her house, and it was gross. Sorry to any Marmite fans out there. Priti's dad joked you have to be born British to like it.

After a *lot* of discussion, we decided to be peace and love instead. I'm going to be wearing a tie-dyed headband and a dress with a peace sign, and Priti is wearing a dress we embellished with a sparkly red heart—because Priti loves to sparkle. Seriously: If peanut butter was sparkly, she would probably eat it!

Well, I better run—I have to finish my homework *and* sewing my twin outfit. Peace out!

"Rise and shine, honey!"

It felt like Zoey had just put down her needle and thread and gone to sleep when her dad came in to wake her up for school. She rubbed her eyes and yawned.

"Were you up late blogging?" Mr. Webber asked.

"No. I had to finish my outfit."

"Well, don't forget you need sleep to finish grow-ing, kiddo." He kissed the top of her head. "Hurry up and get ready. I'll make you bacon and eggs to get you properly fueled."

Zoey jumped out of bed and turned on her laptop to check her blog for comments, like she did every morning. There were more than usual this morning. Most were from her regular readers, responding to the tale of the horrible hat trick and saying that it reminded them of their own struggles in middle school. A Sew Zoey reader named Zigzagger wrote a short but encouraging message:

> Boy, does that bring back memories! Don't worry, it gets better, I promise!

Then she read a comment from CrossStitchGal:

> Remember: This too shall pass. Right now it probably seems like it won't, but trust me, it will. This type of thing happens to a lot of people in middle school, but that doesn't mean it is okay. I

don't know why girls are so mean to each other. Hang in there, honey!

Come to think of it, that was pretty much what the crew members on the set of *Fashion Showdown* told her a while back, when she had been a guest judge. Zoey, aided by the smell of frying bacon wafting up to her bedroom, started to feel more optimistic about the day ahead.

But then she read the next comment, by a reader who had never posted before named Kewlrnu:

Zoey is a TATTLETALE and a FRAUD. She doesn't even make her own clothes!

Zoey looked over at the peace-themed outfit she'd stayed up past her bedtime to finish. How could anyone say she didn't make her own clothes? She shrugged it off. But then she kept reading and saw another post from a new commenter named ZoeySucks:

Who cares about this dumb blog anyway?

These clothes are ugly! I wouldn't even let my mom wear them.

Her blog readers had made criticisms of her sketches before, but they were helpful and constructive, suggesting ways she could make her designs better or easier to construct or pointing out problems that might occur with fabrics. Or saying they didn't love an outfit. No one had ever been straight out . . . mean.

The screen of her laptop quickly grew blurry as Zoey's eyes filled with tears. Knowing there was someone—more than one someone—out there, people she didn't even know, who were willing to write such nasty things made her feel terrible. Who would do such a thing?

"Zooooey!" her dad called from downstairs. "Breakfast!"

Slamming her laptop shut, Zoey jumped up, quickly got dressed in her peace outfit, and ran downstairs. She wasn't even hungry.

"Everything okay?" her dad asked as she sat down at the kitchen table. He placed a heaping plate of bacon and eggs in front of her. "You're looking kind of . . . glum. Eat something?"

Zoey didn't want to talk about it. She wanted today to be a better day than yesterday, and so far it wasn't starting off too promising.

"I'm fine," she said.

"There's nothing a few slices of bacon won't cure," her brother, Marcus, promised, biting into an extra crispy piece.

"I like your style," her dad said. "Groovy!"

"Yeah, the dress is cool," Marcus agreed.

Zoey just hoped her peace-themed outfit would make the rest of her day more peaceful than it had started out.

Kate looked great in her milk bottle costume when Zoey saw her on the bus.

"I can't wait to see you with Libby!" Zoey exclaimed. "You two are going to look awesome together."

"Because of you," Kate said. "Thanks for designing the costumes."

"I loved doing it," Zoey said. "And you helped!"

"Sort of. Hey . . . what happened to your head-band?" Kate asked. "Did it fall off?"

Zoey reached up to her forehead. The tie-dyed headband she had made wasn't there.

"Oh no!" She groaned. "I left it at home! Things were . . . a little crazy this morning."

"It's okay. You still look great without it," Kate assured her.

But Zoey was upset she'd let herself get so flustered about the blog comments that she'd forgotten part of her costume. So far, Spirit Week definitely wasn't going according to plan. Still, she was determined to turn things around. By the time she and Kate got off the bus, Zoey had talked herself into believing that today was going to be a *much* better day than yesterday.

Her faith was shaken when the first people she and Kate encountered when they walked in the school door were Ivy, Shannon, and Bree. They were dressed as triplets, all wearing the same skirts, tops, and hairstyles. Zoey braced herself for the usual snotty remark about her outfit, but to her surprise, Ivy said, "Love your outfit!"

She couldn't believe her ears, especially when Shannon followed up with "So cool!" and Bree chimed in with "Yeah, totally!"

"Uh . . . thanks," Zoey said, edging past them and pulling Kate along with her. As they walked away, Zoey thought she heard Ivy mutter, "Thank *you* for getting us in trouble," but she wasn't completely sure.

Zoey and Kate kept walking in silence until they were out of the line of fire.

"Hey, I thought Backward Day was tomorrow," Kate said. "Why was Ivy being so nice?"

"I don't know," Zoey said. "But maybe she wasn't. I thought I heard her thanking me for getting them in trouble. Did you hear that?"

"No!" Kate exclaimed. "When did she do that?"

"When we were walking away. I think she said it under her breath. Maybe I'm imagining it."

"Careful, Zo," Kate warned. "I don't have a good feeling about this."

"Me neither." Zoey sighed. "But I'm not really sure what I can do about it."

As much as Zoey tried to avoid Ivy, she couldn't

really help seeing her in the classes they had together. But it was Backward Day for the rest of the day, as far as Ivy was concerned. She kept complimenting Zoey at every opportunity.

Even Gabe noticed.

"What's got into Ivy today?" he asked. "She's not usually this nice to you. Actually, she's usually not nice to you at all."

"No idea," Zoey said. She didn't want to start spreading rumors by telling him her suspicions.

"Well, she's right. The peace sign on your dress *is* really awesome. You made it?"

Zoey nodded.

"You're amazing," Gabe said. "Libby said you designed her costume too."

Zoey felt her cheeks flush, and she started picking at a stray thread on her hem.

"I love sewing," she said. "So it doesn't feel like work."

"What, never?" Gabe asked.

"Okay, sometimes it does, especially when I have to do a zipper. But mostly it's fun."

"Too bad homework isn't like that," Gabe said.

"It always feels like work."

Zoey had to agree with him on that.

But it wasn't her homework that ruined Zoey's afternoon. It was reading more mean comments on her blog post when she sat down at her laptop before starting her homework.

Some were from the same posters, Kewlrnu and ZoeySucks, the one who called her clothes ugly. But there were new users, too, saying equally mean things. One named Zzzzzzzoey said her Twin Day designs were "snooze-worthy." All the mean comments were hurtful, but the ones accusing her of not doing her own sewing really stung. She expected her friends to mention the comments, but they hadn't said a word.

Am I being too sensitive? Zoey thought. *Maybe, but every time I check Sew Zoey, there are more awful comments. They can't all be wrong . . . right?*

At dinner that evening, Mr. Webber noticed that Zoey was unusually quiet.

"Is something the matter, honey?" he asked.

Zoey thought about telling her dad about the

nasty comments on her blog. But she was worried that if she did, he might make her stop blogging, and she loved Sew Zoey. She hadn't met most of her regular commenters in real life, and they were all different ages, but despite that she felt like they'd become friends, because they all loved fashion design and sewing. People like Fashionsista gave her encouragement to go on when she felt like giving up. She didn't want to lose all that, just because some people she didn't know were being mean.

"N-no," she said. "Everything's fine."

Her dad and Marcus exchanged glances.

"What?" Zoey asked.

"We're not buying it," Marcus said. "Come on, what is it?"

There were pros and cons of having a family that knew you really well. Zoey didn't want to tell her dad about the comments, so she had to come up with something else.

"Oh, it's just Spirit Week hasn't been as much fun as I thought it would be, that's all," she said.

"Why not?" Mr. Webber asked.

Zoey told them about the hat prank. Marcus

didn't always read her blog posts, but she thought her dad would have seen it.

"I'm pretty sure it was aimed at me, but Libby ended up going home a little early because she was so upset," she said. "It was really unfair."

"There's nothing fair about kids being mean to one another, honey," her dad said.

"I've been looking forward to Spirit Week so much," Zoey said mournfully.

"It's not over yet," Marcus reminded her.

"What's on tap for tomorrow?" her dad asked.

"Backward Day. You have to wear your clothing back to front."

"That seems like it could be very uncomfortable," Mr. Webber said.

"Yeah, especially if you have to go to the bathroom in a hurry," Marcus quipped.

That got a giggle out of Zoey.

"That's why I designed a special dress that *looks* like it's backward but isn't!"

"That's my girl," Mr. Webber said, smiling. "Always one step ahead of everyone."

She wasn't one step ahead of the mean

commenters, though. By the time she sat down to write her evening blog post, there were even more comments, some from the same users and some from even more new users.

Zoey knew she was going to have to do something, but the problem was she didn't know what. She thought about talking to her friends, but they hadn't said anything about the comments, and since she knew they read her blog regularly, maybe that meant she was just overreacting.

When she finished the blog post, Zoey went to her worktable to look over her outfit for the following day. It had a collar on it—backward, of course—but Zoey felt like it needed a little something extra to finish it off. She looked in her sewing box at her collection of ribbon and other trimmings, but nothing was speaking to her.

Just when she was about to give up and go to bed, Zoey's eyes fell on the little tin she used to store buttons.

"That's it!" she said, taking it out of the box. She sifted through the tin until she found four big brightly colored flat buttons. Taking a needle and thread, she sewed them onto the back of the dress.

"Perfect," Zoey said, observing her handiwork. It always made her feel good to find just the right touch to finish off her designs, like putting in the final piece of a jigsaw puzzle.

She couldn't let the people making bad comments take that away from her. But how could she stop them? Zoey decided she'd sleep on it, and maybe she'd figure something out by the morning.

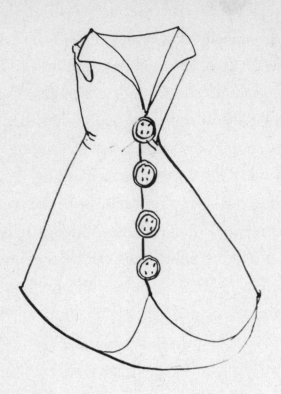

CHAPTER 4

Looking Forward to Dressing Backward!

Spirit Week continues with Backward Day, and then tomorrow will be Decades Day! It's backward to the future. . . . Get it? Anyhoo, I've made an outfit with a backward collar and buttons in the back instead of the front. Pretty crafty, huh? I'm going to wear a long string of beads down my back, although I'll probably have to swing them to the front when I sit in class or else I'll feel like the princess in "The Princess and the Pea," with all those knobbly things distracting me.

I love thinking about clothes being backward. It's totally *looc*! ("cool" spelled backward). It makes me wonder about turning clothes sideways and upside down and inside out and even *slantways* (like the Wonkavator in *Willy Wonka and the Chocolate Factory*). How *looc* would that be?

It's nice to have a fun project to distract me from everything else going on. Life has been feeling pretty back to front at the moment, to tell you the truth. Spirit Week has felt more like Spiritless Week. But at least I've got the karaoke competition on Friday to look forward to. We've got a great dance routine worked out, thanks to Priti, our resident choreographer.

Okay, making it a short and sweet post today. Hoping tomorrow will be sweet too.

Usually Zoey loved checking her blog for comments in the morning before school—the comments from her readers gave her a boost of confidence before she started her day. But not this morning. Not since all the new users had started saying nasty things about her.

This morning she opened her laptop hesitantly, afraid of what she was going to see.

The first few comments were from her regular readers, telling her what a great job she'd done with her Backward Day outfit, which Zigzagger called "inspired" and SewingMama thought was "So backward, it's forward thinking!"

But then . . . there they were. More nasty comments from new Sew Zoey readers.

That purple peace outfit looked like something a cat vomited up.

That's not a peace outfit. That's a freak show outfit. Because Zoey is a freak.

There were replies from Sew Zoey regulars saying that Zoey was absolutely not a freak and that the peace outfit was adorable. Maybe they gave Zoey courage. Maybe it was because she'd had a good night's sleep. Or maybe she'd just had enough. She went to the blog administrator section of her blogging platform. After a little searching, she found out there was a way to block the usernames of the people who were posting the mean comments, so they couldn't comment on Sew Zoey anymore.

There. Done!

Zoey felt better right away, like her blog was her own again. It felt like it was back to the fun, safe, community of friends it had been before. But still, she worried. What if someone believed the lies in those comments? And why did those people hate her blog and her clothes and *her* so much? They didn't even know her!

She'd always been excited to come home from school and check her blog, but now it filled her with dread. She was worrying about her blog problems when she bumped into Priti in the hallway at school.

"Wow, Zo, you're more mopey than my grandmother's bassett hound," Priti said. "Looks like you need a cheerleader, and I know just the person for the job—*me!*"

With that, Priti gave a flamboyant leap, which ended in a dramatic pose, right in the middle of the crowded hallway. Zoey couldn't help laughing. Priti didn't mind if other students were giving her funny looks. She was just herself, and that was enough to cheer up Zoey.

"Oh, you've got to see this!" Priti exclaimed. "I've come up with this amazing tap dance routine I could perform during the bridge part of our karaoke song." She handed her books to Zoey. "Watch, and be amazed!"

Zoey watched, along with a few other students who stopped to stare, as Priti performed a short tap dance routine in the hallway. Everyone clapped when Priti finished with a flourish of jazz hands and tapping feet.

"That *was* amazing," Zoey said to the now panting Priti. "But are you sure you want to take on something new? I'm having a hard time remembering the dance we're doing for the rest of the song."

"It'll be worth it." Priti took her books back from Zoey. "But I still think we need something more to make absolutely sure we win. Wait! I know! Can you do something to make our School Color Day outfits stand out for the karaoke competition?"

Zoey thought for a moment, and then she remembered the fabric in the Holbrookes' spare room closet. "I can make some fab accessories with that sparkly sequin material we found in your hat closet," she said. "Why don't I come home with you after school, and we can start working on them? We can practice the song at the same time."

Priti's smile faded. "No . . . it's okay. My mom and I can drive it over later."

"Why?" Zoey asked. "Maybe I can join you for one of your mom's Indian fusion dinners! I'm still drooling over that calzone thing!"

"No," Priti insisted. "My parents aren't . . . um . . . I mean, my dad has the flu."

Zoey was confused. Mr. Holbrooke seemed fine the other day when they were over at Priti's house, and her friend hadn't mentioned anything about anyone being sick until now. Maybe it was just one of those twenty-four-hour bugs, she thought.

Priti continued, a little less flustered. "You know, I wouldn't want you to catch any flu germs or anything. Especially before our big performance."

"Okay, thanks," Zoey said, realizing that Priti didn't seem to want her to come over. "Tell your dad I hope he feels better."

"Oh . . . sure!" Priti called over her shoulder as she rushed away down the hall, as if she were suddenly and desperately anxious to get to class.

Zoey could see that Priti wasn't acting like her usual upbeat self. Maybe Priti's dad really was sick, but it also seemed like Priti didn't want to talk. Zoey wondered if Priti would confide in her soon or if it was time to ask her if she needed to talk. She wished there was some kind of friendship manual, with all the rules written down like sewing patterns, step by step by step.

Zoey was still thinking about Priti when she passed by Ivy, Bree, and Shannon in the hallway between classes.

"Hey, Zoey," Shannon said, waving to her. "How'd you do your hair like that?"

Zoey had done her hair in a backward—or, well, upside down—French braid, in honor of Backward

Day. She spoke cautiously, bracing for a snide remark to whatever answer she gave. "Why?"

"It's cool!" Shannon replied.

"Yeah, actually, it is," added Bree. "Can you show us how to do it?"

"We won't bite," Ivy said, seeing Zoey's puzzled expression.

Now Zoey was really confused. Had aliens arrived at Mapleton Prep and switched the mean girls with nice ones? Were they just being on their best behavior because of Ms. Austen's warning? Somehow, Zoey decided, this felt genuine, so she decided to give them the benefit of the doubt.

"Well?" Ivy asked.

"I saw a how-to video online," Zoey said. "I think they called it an upside-down French braid."

"It looks complicated," Shannon said.

Zoey paused. "Not really. You just start braiding from the back of your head, by your neck, and then work your way up to your forehead. Look it up online."

"Thanks!" Bree said.

"Yeah, thanks, Zoey," Shannon piped in.

Zoey walked away, thinking about what had just happened. Shannon was Zoey's friend in elementary school, and sometimes she was still nice to Zoey when Ivy and Bree weren't around. But she wouldn't usually be nice to Zoey in front of Bree or Ivy. What was going on? Did they really just like her hair? Being nice wasn't their style.

Zoey was distracted on the bus ride home. She almost didn't care about the trio of girls at school anymore when she thought about what had happened recently on Sew Zoey. People she didn't even know had written in to say that they didn't like her clothes and that she was a joke. She hoped that blocking the users would make a difference, and it felt good to do something. But was holding her breath on the way home, waiting to see what would happen when she checked her blog again.

"What's the matter, Zo?" Kate asked. "You're in la-la land. Did you hear a thing I just said?"

"I'm sorry." Zoey sighed. "I just . . . I'm really upset about these comments that keep showing up on my blog. Really nasty ones. More every day."

"Oh! I saw those. They were awful!" Kate exclaimed. "But since you didn't mention them I thought they weren't bothering you. Who would write something like that?"

"I don't know. That's the problem. But it's really starting to freak me out. I thought they would stop, but it just keeps getting worse. I kind of thought I was being too sensitive since you and Priti didn't say anything, but I guess not."

"Have you talked to your dad?" Kate asked.

"No," Zoey confessed. "I'm afraid if I do, he'll overreact and make me shut down the whole blog."

Kate frowned. "Are you sure? Maybe he'll just know how to help without making you do that."

Zoey shook her head.

"Remember the fight you and I got into the last time he got worried about what was happening on my blog? You thought I was mad at you and was deleting your name on purpose, but it was actually my dad deleting names to protect our privacy."

"Oh yeah," Kate said. "Maybe you're right."

"This morning, I blocked all the commenters who wrote nasty stuff, so hopefully there won't be any when I check after I get home. I hope it works. Other than doing that, I don't know what to do."

"If it were me, I'd take a soccer ball outside and kick it around until I felt better," Kate said. "Sometimes I find just messing around with the ball helps me find the answer."

Zoey laughed. "You know me, Kate. I'm totally sports challenged. If I tried doing that, I'd just end up getting *more* frustrated and upset! And probably hurt!"

Kate grinned. "I guess. Well, at least you aren't having crush problems. That's what I thought you were upset about."

Zoey hadn't even thought about her crush on Lorenzo. Or about how Gabe was kind of cute too. Well, maybe she'd thought about that a little bit when he'd been wearing his great-grandfather's top hat. But she'd had too much else on her mind.

"I've got other things to worry about right now," she said.

"Why don't we tell everyone else at lunch tomorrow?" Kate suggested. "Maybe they'll have some good ideas. I bet they will, you know?"

Zoey thought that was a good plan, because she already felt a little better now that she and Kate had talked.

But the feeling was short lived. When she got home and checked her blog, there were more mean comments. . . . This time from new readers. As soon as she blocked one username, it seemed, another person would spring up and write something even nastier. It was starting to feel like the world was full of people who didn't like her or Sew Zoey. It made her feel horrible and small and alone.

At least she had Marcus's band practice to distract her. They were all down in the basement, practicing their usual stuff, but Marcus had promised they would play her karaoke song so she could practice. Zoey went downstairs and sat on the bottom step, waiting patiently until the band finished the song they were playing.

"Hey, Zoey," said Marcus's friend Dan, who played guitar. "You ready?"

Ralph, the lead singer, handed Zoey his microphone. "Over to you, Zo," he said.

Marcus tapped out the opening on his sticks

and they started playing. Zoey was distracted from thinking about the comments and missed the first cue. They had to start over. Ralph offered to cue her.

"But you won't be there on Friday," Zoey wailed. "I need to get it right by myself."

"It's okay," Ralph said. "Just this one time, and then you'll get it."

They started over, and this time Zoey kept her eyes on Ralph and her mind on the song and came in right when she should.

> *"You are you and I am me*
> *And that's the way it*
> *All should be*
> *'Cause no one should*
> *Have to pretend*
> *For us to be*
> *The best of friends . . ."*

They ran through the song twice, and after the second time, Zoey felt much more confident. She stayed and listened to the band practice until Mr. Webber shouted down to say that Priti was at the door. Zoey ran upstairs to meet her.

"Here's the fabric," Priti said, handing a plastic bag to Zoey.

"Thanks," Zoey said. "Guess what? I just practiced our song with Marcus's band! Wanna join us?"

"Fun! I wish I could, but my mom's waiting."

Mrs. Holbrooke honked the horn twice, clearly impatient. Priti's smile dimmed, but only for a second.

"Got to run. Make us awesome stuff!" Priti shouted as she ran to her mom's car.

"I will!" Zoey called after her.

As Zoey went inside, she wondered again what was going on with Priti and her family. She hoped Priti would confide in her soon.

Upstairs in her room, Zoey decided to check her blog before working on ideas for the accessories. *Maybe it'll be better this time,* she thought as she scrolled through the comments.

Nothing over-the-top bad! Did the blocking really work?

Then she refreshed the page, and a new user comment popped up.

Sew Zoey? Sew stupid.

Zoey blocked the user, saying good-bye as she clicked on the button. *I am so tired of this,* she thought. *Why does everyone hate me?*

She felt so gloomy, she almost didn't check her e-mail—but was she ever glad she did! Because there, in her in-box, was an e-mail from the online editor of *Très Chic,* her favorite magazine:

Dear Sew Zoey,

I'm the online editor at *Très Chic* magazine's website, and I'm writing to see if you would be interested in participating in a special feature for our online edition. We're doing a series of kid-focused "Day in the Life of a Designer" interviews and would like to include you and your blog!

If you're interested, we'll send a reporter and a photographer to your town to shadow you as you go about your day, work on sewing projects, etc. You'll have to get permission from your parents and your school, of course, and have them sign release forms.

I'm attaching a list of other young fashion designers we're approaching for the piece. You're in good company! You might know of Allie Lovallo? She has an accessory design blog, Always Allie Accessories. If you can think of other young designers of your caliber that should be included on the list, please let me know!

So, that's all for now. I do hope you're up for it. It wouldn't be a good feature about young designers without you!

Best wishes,

Isabella Caminelli

PS Please feel free to call me Izzy!

Whoa! Zoey didn't dare touch her computer at first, for fear that the whole e-mail was a dream and would vanish into thin air if she closed the screen. So she blinked her eyes a few times. . . . And when she opened them, the e-mail was still there. And "Call Me Izzy" had an e-mail address that ended in @treschiczine.com, which seemed pretty legitimate. Now Zoey was beyond excited! She had really needed some good news right at that very moment, but she never would have expected that she would get the best news: the chance to be in a feature on the online edition of her favorite magazine of all time. Did people at *Très Chic* really know about Sew Zoey? Was it because of her appearance on *Fashion Showdown*?

She was almost more excited to know there were so many other kids who were interested in designing and sewing. Not everyone on the list had a blog, but a few of them did, including Allie Lovallo. She checked out Allie's blog, and her handbag, headband, and jewelry designs were really cute. When she read the About Me section, she saw that Allie lived not too far from Zoey. *I wonder if Allie ever has to deal with mean comments on her blog?* Zoey thought. Just thinking about it made her feel less alone.

Zoey wrote a quick reply to say she had to ask her dad first, but that if he agreed, it would be her dream come true to be in the feature. The editor wrote back straightaway with the parent and school release forms and asked Zoey to return them as soon as possible if she was interested in being a part of the feature.

Was she interested? Definitely! Zoey printed out the e-mail and permission form and headed downstairs to find her dad. He was in the living room watching a football game and making a grocery list at the same time.

"Hey, Dad! Guess what! *Très Chic* wants to do a feature on me for their online edition!" Zoey said, handing him the e-mail from the editor.

Mr. Webber read it and smiled up at his daughter. "Wow, fame just keeps on knocking at your door, eh, Zoey?"

Zoey thought about the mean comments on her blog. Fame wasn't the only thing that was knocking on her door.

"I guess so," she said. "Anyway, they need your permission."

Zoey gave her dad the permission forms.

"If you are up for it, I'm up for it!"

Normally, Zoey wouldn't have hesitated, but she did wonder for a second if being in the feature would make more people discover Sew Zoey and write awful things about it. But only for a second. Then she decided that whatever happened, this would be worth it. There was no way she was going to let some stupid comments stop her from doing something she really loved. No way.

"Definitely!"

"Okey-dokey! I'll sign, scan, and e-mail it back to them tonight before I go to bed," her dad said. "You know, things are going to be busy for a while with the championship games coming up . . . so this is perfect timing. I'm so proud of you, Zoey."

"Thanks, Dad." Zoey hugged her father before going back up to her room, taking the stairs two at a time, filled with a new energy.

She spread the sparkly, sequined material out on her worktable. It caught the light and shimmered with possibility as it settled on the flat surface. How could she best use it to make accessories for the four friends?

Zoey measured the material carefully to see how much of it she had. Then she got out her sketch-book, flopped onto her bed, and started playing with ideas, trying to figure out how many things she'd be able to make with the length of fabric.

When she was satisfied, she went to the closet and moved her own clothes aside to get to the section where she kept her mother's designs. Tomorrow was Decades Day, and Zoey was going to wear one of her mother's dresses for her nineties outfit. She hung the dress on the outside of her closet door and wondered what her mom would say about the comments on her blog, how she would tell Zoey to deal with them.

It's not like she could ever know. She could only imagine.

Zoey wasn't one to mope for long. She knew she would always have her dad, Marcus, Aunt Lulu, and her friends to back her up if she ever really needed it. She also had all the online friends and supporters she'd made through Sew Zoey. And she had a blog post to write for them before she went to bed!

CHAPTER 5

Time Travel ... Fashion Style!

It's Decades Day and between us, my friends and I are spanning the last four decades of the twentieth century. Libby's going to be a sixties flower child; Priti's going full-on seventies disco, complete with platform shoes and as many shiny, plasticky fabrics as she can find in her house; and Kate has got the absolutely perfect outfit for herself—she found an old Jane Fonda workout video at her grandma's house and she's going to dress like the original eighties home exercise video queen, with a leotard and tights and big leg warmers. As for me, I'm going to dress like my mom did in high school, or so Aunt Lulu tells me—nineties grunge. Aunt Lulu says by today's standards, it wasn't a great look, but it's growing on me. I'm wearing one of Mom's designs, and Aunt Lulu loaned me her black Doc Martens, which fit if I wear really thick socks, but that's okay because the socks kind of complete the look, anyway.

Ooooh! GUESS WHAT?! I can't believe I managed to get halfway through the blog post before I spilled this news! I got an e-mail yesterday from the online editor of my absolute favorite magazine, *Très Chic*, and they want to do a profile on me for a special "Day in the Life of a Designer" piece about young designers! Crazy, right?

I know what you're thinking: Is this for real? Yes, it's for real! Your eyes aren't playing tricks on you. I'm going to be in *Très Chic*!!

They're sending a reporter and a photographer

to follow me around for a day, at home and at school. I'm so excited! And also a little nervous. But mostly excited!

"Great Doc Martens," Gabe said, when Zoey sat behind him in English the next morning. "And your dress is really pretty."

"It's my mom's," Zoey said. "She made it."

"Oh, so your mom is into sewing too?" he said. "I guess that's where you get it from. I bet she's really proud of you, huh?"

Zoey didn't know how to respond. Obviously, Gabe didn't know her mom died when she was little. She thought everyone knew—that it was an accepted part of her identity, just like she was Zoey Webber, the girl who had a fashion blog.

"Uh, yeah," she said, but she didn't tell him she only knew that because her father and Aunt Lulu told her that her mom would have been. She figured it would have just made it awkward for both of them.

But it made her feel unsettled for the rest of the

morning. Libby could tell something was up as soon as she sat down at the lunch table.

"What's the matter, Zoey?" she asked.

Kate didn't know about the Gabe incident, but she gave Zoey a meaningful look, urging her to tell Libby and Priti about her blog problems, as they'd talked about on the bus yesterday.

"I've been having problems on Sew Zoey," Zoey said. "There are a bunch of new readers, and they've been posting some really mean things."

"Like what?" Priti asked. "I haven't been on the last day or two."

"Saying that I'm a fraud and I don't even sew my own designs."

"What?!" Libby exclaimed. "That's ridiculous! Everyone knows you do."

"Of course *we* know it," Kate said. "Because we *know* Zoey. But *they* don't—the people on the Internet who don't actually know Zoey for real."

"They've said lots of other horrible stuff about my designs," Zoey said. "I finally started blocking people so they can't add comments. But it seems like as soon as I block one user, a new one pops up."

"Do you think it's you know who and friends?" Priti asked.

"I don't know," Zoey sighed. "I have no way of telling. Besides, there are a lot of new users, not just three. I've lost count. It feels like everyone is out to get me. Since when is there a We Hate Sew Zoey fan club?"

"There's got to be some way of finding out who is doing it," Libby said.

"Ivy's been supernice in school since Ms. Austen gave them all a warning," Zoey said. "So I don't think it's her. . . ."

"I wonder how long that's going to last," Kate remarked.

"Me too," Priti said.

"Me three," Zoey said. "Because it's not going to last forever."

It didn't.

Later that afternoon, Zoey came around the corner of the hallway and bumped into you know who herself, trailed by Shannon and Bree. They were all dressed as punk rockers. Ivy had a fake pink wig and safety pin earrings.

"That dress looks like it's ready for the rag pile," Bree said.

"I know, right?" Shannon agreed.

"Totally. It's hideous," Ivy said. "I would never wear that rag to school. Or those horrible mannish boots."

"They're called Doc Martens," Zoey said, trying to control the shaking in her voice. "As a matter of fact, a lot of *female* punk rockers wore them."

She walked away, ignoring the laughter and snide comments that followed her.

It was bad enough that Ivy made comments about Aunt Lulu's boots. But how dare she insult her mom's dress? That hurt Zoey in an even deeper place.

She was still upset about it when Libby's mom dropped off the girls at The Perfect Ten to get their nails painted in the school colors for the grand finale of Spirit Week. Friday was School Colors Day, and the whole school would be gathering in the auditorium to watch the karaoke competition.

"I'm so excited for tomorrow," Priti said. "We're totally going to win. I'm sure. Especially now that Zoey is making accessories for our outfits."

"She is?" Kate said. "Can't wait to see them!"

"Well, they're not ready yet," Zoey said. "But I've got the designs all worked out."

"She's using that cool material we found in the hat closet," Priti said.

"Let's put a top coat of glitter polish on our nails to match," Libby suggested.

"Great idea!" Priti exclaimed. "Or maybe just glitter on the tips . . . like a sparkly French manicure."

"You're asking for *less* sparkle?" Zoey asked Priti. "Who are you and what have you done with my friend?"

Priti laughed. "Very funny, Zo. But, seriously, wouldn't that look cool?"

Kate, whose style was usually a little more understated—and whose mom was a little more conservative when it came to fashion—wasn't quite as enthusiastic.

"Do we have to add glitter polish? It's going to

be weird enough to have my nails painted red and silver without having them sparkle, too."

Kate's usual nail color pick was a barely there pink, and even then she usually took it off within a day or two.

"Come on, Kate! It's only for one day. You can take it off tomorrow night if it bothers you," Priti coaxed.

"Okay." Kate sighed. "I guess I'll have to take some sparkles for the team," she said.

"That's our girl," Zoey said. "Always a team player."

When their nails were dry, Libby's mom drove them to the Flynn house for a final rehearsal of their karaoke routine.

While Libby was searching for "Be Yourself" on her MP3 player, Zoey told her friends about what Ivy said about her mom's dress.

"Why would she say something like that?" Kate exclaimed. "I don't get it!"

"That's because you're nice," Zoey replied. "Your life's mission isn't to make someone else miserable."

"I don't understand why she always seems to pick on you," Priti said. "What have you ever done to her?"

"Nothing," Zoey said. "At least nothing I know of. I try to ignore her like everyone says. 'If you don't react, she'll stop.' But she doesn't. She keeps going. If anything, she's getting worse."

"Zo, I know you don't want to tell your dad about what's been going on, but I think you should," Kate said, her brow creased with concern.

"Kate's right," Libby said. "It's out of control."

"But don't you think that'll just make things worse?" Zoey asked.

"She's already making you miserable," Priti pointed out. "How can it get much worse?"

Zoey could think of plenty of ways. But she started to think maybe her friends were right and it *was* time to talk to her dad.

"I guess I'll talk to him when he gets home tonight," she said. "I just hope he doesn't go overboard—you know, going to see Ms. Austen and making me shut down Sew Zoey. That would be worse thing ever."

"I can think of something worse," Priti said quietly.

"What?" Zoey asked, exchanging concerned looks with Kate and Libby, as if to say, *Did you hear that?*

Priti's expression changed from downcast to perky in a flash. "Oh, who knows!" Priti said. "I'm just being dramatic. Forget about it. You know, we really need to practice our karaoke routine. Especially since Ivy, Bree, and Shannon are competing, too, and we don't want to lose to them!"

That would *be the worst,* Zoey thought. She didn't want to lose to anyone, but beating those girls was a matter of pride.

"No way!" Libby said. "Come on, let's do it!"

Priti grabbed Kate's and Zoey's hands, dragging them onto the imaginary stage. They practiced the routine for an hour, stopping when Mrs. Flynn brought them milk and cookies to keep them going. Then she sat on the sofa to be their audience for another run-through.

She clapped loudly when they finished.

"Great job!" she said. "I'd run through the dance

sequence in the bridge one more time—that's the only part that's a little shaky."

Priti made them run through it five more times, not just once. Zoey was exhausted and starving for dinner by the time Mrs. Mackey came to drive her and Kate home.

"My feet hurt," Zoey complained as she slid into the backseat of the car. "I still have to make the accessories tonight too."

"Do you want me to come over and help after I finish my homework?" Kate asked.

"Yes, please!" Zoey yawned. "I'm not sure I'll get them all done otherwise."

Zoey called for her dad as soon as she walked in the door, hoping to talk to him about the Ivy situation before dinner. She got Marcus instead.

"Dad's not here," he said. "He had to work late again. He said to say sorry it's been such a crazy week. I'm going to order pizza from Villa Camillo. Do you want any extras? Garlic knots? Salad? Toppings?"

"No." Zoey sighed. Now that she'd made the decision to tell her dad her problems, she wanted to talk to him. Now. Tonight. Before anything made her change her mind about it.

"You okay?" Marcus asked.

"Yeah. Just tired," Zoey said. "And I have to make accessories for tomorrow. Kate's coming over later to help."

"Okay—you go sew. I'll give you a shout when the food gets here."

Zoey dragged herself up to her room, tired and miserable. She'd been so looking forward to Spirit Week, but instead of boosting her spirits, it had left her down in the dumps.

She turned on her laptop to check her blog and her e-mail before she started cutting fabric for the accessories.

There were more nasty comments on her blog from usernames she didn't recognize.

Zoey had enough. She went to the administrator page to block the new users. This time she saw that there was a way to delete the blocked user comments from her blog. She pressed delete and breathed a sigh of relief. When she looked back at her blog, the mean comments were gone.

At least all her regular readers were supportive of her, telling her she was right to block the users who weren't being constructive. Still, Zoey wished she didn't have to deal with blocking anyone at all.

Her e-mail, at least, brought her quite a nice surprise—a note from Allie Lovallo, the teen who lived nearby and wrote the Always Allie Accessories blog. She said she was soooooooooo excited about the *Très Chic* feature and asked Zoey if she wanted to meet. Best of all, she suggested meeting at A Stitch in Time because it was her favorite store!

Zoey wrote back:

> I'd love to meet you! A Stitch in Time is my favorite store too! I have to check with my dad though, because I don't have my license yet since I'm only in 7th grade. Maybe this weekend?

She pressed send and then went to her worktable and picked up her scissors. Working carefully from the patterns she'd made from her designs the night before, she cut the material for four scarves, four cuff bracelets, and four small fascinators to go in each of her friends' ponytails.

The fascinators were going to be the most fiddly, so Zoey got to work on those first. She could have Kate hem the scarves when she came over later.

Zoey was so involved with carefully sewing the sequin fabric around the wire structures she'd created that she didn't even hear Marcus calling her to tell her the pizza arrived. When he burst into her room, she was so surprised, she pricked her finger.

"Ouch! You scared me!"

"Didn't you hear me shouting?" Marcus asked.

"No. I was trying to make sure the fabric sat flat instead of puckering."

"So your ears don't work when you're sewing?" Marcus asked with a grin.

"I was *concentrating*," Zoey explained, putting down the fascinator she was working on.

"Well, come concentrate on dinner before the pizza gets cold."

Over dinner, Zoey told Marcus about Allie's e-mail.

"I can drive you if Dad's busy," he said. "As long as he says it's okay for you to go meet some random girl off the Internet."

"She's not *random*," Zoey argued. "She's going to be in *Très Chic*'s online feature on teen designers. Just like me."

"Whatever. You haven't met her before and Dad needs to say it's okay."

"I know," Zoey said, taking a bite of pizza.

The doorbell rang. Zoey started to get up, but Marcus said, "Finish your slice. I'll get it."

He came back in with Kate.

"I'm done," Zoey said, getting up and putting her plate in the dishwasher. "Can't wait to show you the fascinators!"

After Kate ate a slice of pizza—she was always game for a snack—they went to Zoey's room to look at the hats.

"Wow, these are amazing!" Kate said. "How did you do that?"

"Not easily!" Zoey admitted. "They were a lot harder than I thought they'd be. It's taken me forever just to do three because I couldn't get the fabric to lie flat. And I still have all the other things to make."

"That's what I'm here for!" Kate said. "What can I do to help?"

"How about you cut out the pattern for the wrist cuffs while I finish this last fascinator, and then the scarves are easy-peasy."

"Sounds like a plan!" Kate declared.

Zoey put on music and they both got to work.

"It's true what they say about many hands make light work," Zoey said when they were almost finished. "I thought I was going to be up all night!"

Mr. Webber popped his head into Zoey's bedroom.

"Hi, honey—hi, Kate. Sorry I wasn't home for dinner. Had to do some extra rehab with some injured players to try to get them back in playing form for the championships."

"It's okay," Zoey said. "Marcus ordered pizza."

"Marcus said you have a question for me?" her dad went on.

Zoey explained that Allie from the *Très Chic* online feature wanted to meet her at A Stitch in

Time. Her dad agreed, as long as he could talk to Allie's parents first and stay at the fabric store with them during the meet up. "You know, I'm sure if the folks at *Très Chic* give Allie their seal of approval, there's nothing to worry about . . . but you can't be too careful."

"Thanks, Dad!" Zoey said.

Her dad scanned the room. "What are you two up to?"

"Kate's helping me make accessories for tomorrow," she said. "You know, for the karaoke competition."

Mr. Webber came in and picked up one of the fascinators, but held it upside down.

"Wow. This is cool. What is it, exactly?"

"It's a *fascinator*, Dad," Zoey said.

"Well, that's absolutely *fascinating*, but I still don't understand what it is," her dad said.

"You wear it in your hair," Kate explained.

Mr. Webber held up the sparkly fascinator to his thinning hairline.

"You mean like *this*?"

Kate giggled. Zoey rolled her eyes.

"Um . . . no!" she said. "You should stick to base-ball hats."

"Right now, I think I'll forego hats of any kind," Zoey's dad replied, "in favor of a long, hot shower. Good night, girls."

He gave Zoey a kiss on the forehead. Zoey was thinking of asking him to wait so she could talk with him when a car horn honked outside. First once, then two more times. When she looked back for her dad, he was gone.

"That must be my mom," Kate said. "Time to go . . ."

"Thanks for helping me, Kate," Zoey said. "I wouldn't have finished otherwise."

"We're a team, right?" Kate said. She waved her nails in Zoey's face. "A very *sparkly* team!"

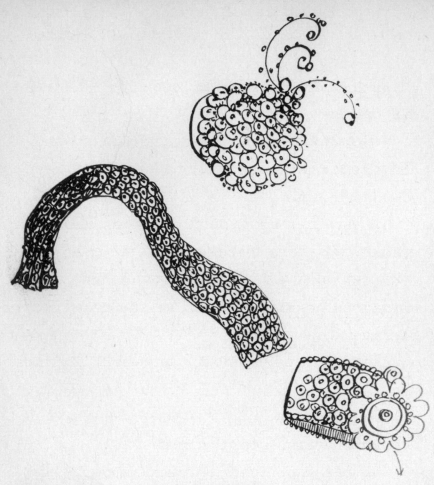

CHAPTER 6

Glitter Up, Girls!

I never thought I'd say this, because I ❤ Mapleton Prep and I'm usually full of school spirit, but TGIF! I'm sooooo glad Spirit Week is almost over. It hasn't turned out to be nearly as much fun as I thought it would be. You know when you've looked forward to something for a long time, and then it doesn't quite live up to your expectations? Yup. Like that.

Maybe today, School Colors Day, will be the day that turns it all around. I'm really happy with how the accessories I made last night (with help from Kate, thank you, sparkly teammate!!) came out. How do you spice up School Colors Day? Add sequins! We found some sequined material in the hat closet at Priti's house when we were looking at hats. Priti said I could use it, and I tried to work it as little as possible so nothing went to waste, because it's so beautiful and sparkly! It'll give our outfits the perfect finishing touch when it's time for the karaoke competition, don't you think?

Now if we can only remember all the dance moves and the words to our song! Wish me—oops! I mean, wish *us*—luck!

The entrance to Mapleton Prep was a sea of red and silver when Kate and Zoey got off the bus the next morning.

Morning classes passed quickly because they were on an abbreviated schedule so the students could finish early for the school assembly.

Kate, Libby, Priti, and Zoey met in the girls' bathroom before the assembly to get dressed for the karaoke competition. Zoey had a shopping bag full of sparkly accessories to add to their School Colors Day outfits.

"What do you think?" she asked, putting a fascinator on Libby first. "Does this look right?"

"Perfect, totally, yes! And I love what you did with the fabric!" Priti exclaimed, practically bouncing with excitement. "Where's mine? I can't wait to put it on!"

Zoey took it out and helped Priti put it in her hair. Kate gave Priti a scarf and wrist cuffs. Priti wrapped the scarf around her neck and tossed the ends over her shoulder with a jaunty flair.

"These accessories are so cool!" Libby said, snapping on some wrist cuffs. "You must have been up all night, Zoey."

"No, Kate helped me," Zoey said. "Otherwise I totally *would* have been up all night."

Soon after, the entire school gathered in the auditorium for the Spirit Assembly and karaoke competition. There was red and silver everywhere!

"Thank you for all the creativity you've displayed this week," Ms. Austen told the students. "I've been so impressed by the outfits you've come up with for each of our Spirit Week theme days."

She picked up the remote for the projector.

"Let's have a look at some of the great ensembles we've seen in school this week," she said, starting a slideshow.

Zoey grabbed Kate when a picture of Kate and Libby in their Oreos and milk costume came up. "Look! It's you!"

There also was a picture of Priti in her Decades Day costume, and Zoey in her Backward Day outfit.

"Do you think any of these will end up in the yearbook?" Kate whispered.

"Maybe!" Zoey said.

When the slideshow ended, Ms. Austen said it was time to announce the Spirit Week prizes. Zoey's heart started to beat a little faster. It had been a challenging week, what with all the unpleasant stuff on her blog, and winning a prize for best costume would definitely cheer her up.

But as Ms. Austen went down the list of prizes, her name wasn't called. Not once. Zoey wondered if maybe, just maybe, the comments on her blog about her having no talent were just saying the truth.

"And now, last, but definitely not least, Best Team Costume," Ms. Austen announced. She paused a moment for dramatic effect. "Libby Flynn and Kate Mackey for milk and Oreos!"

Kate jumped up with an excited squeal, and Libby was out of her seat, embracing Kate, then Priti, and then Zoey on the way to pick up their prize certificates. Zoey was happy to cheer for her friends, and especially thrilled to see Libby with such a radiant smile on her face after the horrible Hat Day incident. As she and Kate walked back to their seats, Libby got extra loud cheers from her classmates in Mrs. Brennan's class. At least something was going right in the world, Zoey thought.

"This is kind of your award too," Kate said, giving Zoey a hug as she sat down. "After all, you designed the costumes."

Zoey smiled, glad she had friends who appreciated her, but she was preoccupied by her nerves.

"Thanks," she said. "Right now, I'm worried about remembering the dance steps!"

"You'll be fine," Kate assured her. "You're an old pro at this now. After you've been on TV, doing karaoke in school should be a piece of cake!"

But as the karaoke contest began, Zoey got more and more nervous. The competition was really good. She never realized how many good singers there were at Mapleton Prep. Zoey knew she sounded okay in the shower, but it was different when she sang with a microphone. People could hear her! Priti had a great voice, and Libby's was pretty good, but she and Kate were better dancers than singers. Hopefully, their fancy footwork would wow the audience enough to make up for their so-so vocals.

There were a few groups who went first and got a decent amount of applause from the crowd. Then it was time for Ivy, Shannon, and Bree to sing. The music started and Zoey and her friends gasped.

"You are you and I am me
And that's the way it
All should be . . ."

They were singing "Be Yourself" by Las Chicas!

"Oh my gosh," Zoey whispered to Kate, Priti, and Libby. "They're singing our song!"

Libby's lip began to quiver. "Everyone's going to think we're copying them!" she said.

"I don't get it," Kate whispered back. "They're not really about 'being yourself,' you know? Why would they pick *that* song?"

"Hold on." Zoey thought back to gym class earlier in the week. "I heard them say they were going to sing "Get Your Cool On." Why would they switch songs?"

"I'm sorry to say this, but maybe they knew we chose that song and wanted to mess with us," Priti said in a hushed voice. "But how did they know?"

Kate shrugged.

"Oh no!" Zoey said. "I think . . . I think I wrote about it in my blog."

For a moment, all four girls were quiet.

Then Libby asked, "What are we going to do?"

Priti sat up straighter and put on her best pep-talk voice. "We're going to go out there and give it our best. I refuse to let them win!"

Zoey smiled. That was so very Priti. The girls nodded in agreement and waited for the song to end.

Zoey wanted to hate Ivy, Bree, and Shannon's performance, but she had to admit they did pretty well, and they certainly got a decent amount of applause from the crowd. As the clapping petered out, Ms. Austen spoke again.

"Nice singing, girls. Okay, next up, we've got Priti Holbrooke, Libby Flynn, Kate Mackey, and Zoey Webber!" Ms. Austen said. "And . . . oh . . . it looks like they're also singing 'Be Yourself.' Great minds think alike!"

Zoey heard whispers coming from the audience as they walked up to the stage.

"Quiet, everyone," Ms. Austen said.

It's going to be fine, Zoey told herself as got into position. If I can handle Fashion Showdown, I can totally handle this.

But when the music started, Zoey stood frozen in place for what felt like an eternity. When she saw the familiar faces in the crowd—particularly Lorenzo's face—her mind went completely blank.

She looked over at Priti, Libby, and Kate: They were getting into the music and seemed to be actually having fun. *Maybe I can just sneak offstage and no one will notice,* Zoey thought.

She wished the floor would open up and make her disappear—until she caught sight of both Gabe and Ms. Austen smiling and nodding at her encouragingly, as if to say, *Come on, Zoey, you can do this!*

That was enough to make her snap out of it.

Glancing at Priti, she was able to pick up exactly where they were in the dance, and she rocked the rest of the song and the dance routine.

What's more, she actually had fun!

When the music stopped, the whole auditorium jumped to their feet and started to clap wildly.

"Nice job," Ms. Austen said as they walked off the stage.

Gabe smiled at Zoey and gave her a high five as she walked by.

When they reached their seats and sat down, Kate, Priti, and Libby looked visibly relieved. Zoey was still reeling from her episode of stage fright.

"I can't believe I froze like that," Zoey said. "Did it totally ruin everything?"

"People barely noticed," Priti said. "It was only for, like, two seconds."

"Two seconds!" Zoey exclaimed. "It felt like an hour!"

"It might have *felt* like an hour, but it wasn't," Libby said. "It just looked like you hesitated for a second or two."

"Whew! So I didn't look like a complete dork." Zoey sighed in relief. "And I think they liked us a little better than Ivy's group."

"Absolutely," Priti said.

"Good job, guys!" Kate added. "We showed them!"

It still wasn't enough to win the competition, though. A group of eighth graders came in first place. But then Ms. Austen said she had an impromptu award to give out.

"I was so impressed with the razzle-dazzle accessories worn by Priti, Libby, Zoey, and Kate, that I'm giving them the Most Pizzazz award," she announced.

Zoey practically skipped up the aisle with the others to get her certificate, which Ms. Austen had hastily written out backstage. She was excited to have won *something* for her original designs. She knew she hadn't put in her best effort this week because of all the distractions on her blog, but sewing was her thing, so it would have been really disappointing not to win anything at all.

"Today turned out to be fun, but I am *so glad* this week is over!" Zoey confessed to Kate on the bus home.

"I know. It's been a tough week for you. Did you get to speak to your dad last night?"

"No," Zoey said, moaning. "He really did take a long shower. I guess I fell asleep. And I didn't want to bother him."

"You have to talk to him over the weekend, Zo," Kate said. "Especially if there are more comments."

"I know," Zoey said. "It's gotten to the point where I dread going home to check my blog instead of looking forward to it—and that's totally cray, right?"

"Seriously cray," Kate agreed.

"I'll definitely talk to Dad," Zoey promised.

When she got home, Zoey had a snack and then went up to her room to get her laptop. She felt a sense of foreboding as she clicked on the shortcut for her blog.

The first few comments were from her usual readers, complimenting her on the accessories and asking how the karaoke competition went. But then . . . more mean comments! Really mean ones. So mean that Zoey slammed her laptop shut. She didn't want to read any more of them. She didn't want to even look at her blog. It had always been fun, but now it wasn't.

This isn't going away, Zoey thought. *It's getting worse. Why do people I don't even know hate me so much?*

It was definitely time to talk to her father.

This was too big for her to handle by herself.

---------- CHAPTER 7 ----------

To Blog or Not to Blog

I hate to admit it, but I'm glad Spirit Week is over. That sounds very spiritless of me, doesn't it? Thanks for asking about the karaoke contest. After a moment that seemed like an hour of me completely freezing up, I pulled myself together and had a great time. I might not be the best singer in the world, but between us, we make a great group. We didn't win the karaoke competition, but we *did* win an award for Most Pizzazz for our sparkletastic accessories. That made me feel pretty good, and Kate and Libby won Best Team Costume for the Oreos and milk costume, which was awesome too.

But to tell you the truth, this week has been kind of crummy—mostly because of what's been taking place right here on Sew Zoey. I'm feeling pretty blogged out, and it's made me think seriously about if I even want to keep blogging at all. That question is the inspiration for today's clothing sketches. Don't get me wrong—I *love* this blog, and I've learned so much from the feedback and the comments you've posted. You inspire me to try new things and to work harder, and you've helped me find solutions to sewing problems—and sometimes even to middle school ones, too!

But you might have noticed there have been some new readers on the blog, and a bunch of comments that . . . well . . . aren't very nice. That's actually putting it mildly. Some of them have been really, *really* mean. I've thought about it, and while I know it's a free country and we have a right to free speech and all that, this is my blog, so I get to set the rules. Like Dad says if Marcus and I argue with him when he's laid down the law about something, "This country might be a democracy, but this house isn't."

So here they are—and there are only two, so it's not like I'm getting too bossy or anything, I hope:

1. Sew Zoey welcomes constructive criticism, but nasty comments will be deleted.

2. Users who write nasty comments will be blocked.

I think that's fair, don't you? We should all be able to come here without having to worry about people being mean. It's bad enough having to deal with that at school.

Zoey spent Friday night curled up on the sofa, watching movies and worrying. What if the people from *Très Chic* read her blog and started to believe the stuff the mean commenters wrote? What if they thought she really *was* a fraud who didn't design and sew her own clothes and decided not to include her in the online feature? It would be so awful to be cut when none of that was even true!

Maybe she should just take a break from Sew Zoey. Or just stop doing it, period.

But the thought of not doing Sew Zoey made her even sadder than the nasty comments. In the short time since she started the blog, so many great things had come from it. She had a secret fashion fairy godmother, Fashionsista, who was an amazing mentor and, even more than that, a friend who sent her encouraging notes and gifts. She'd been invited to be a guest judge on her favorite TV show, *Fashion Showdown*. And now, she was about to be part of a feature on teen designers in her absolute favorite fashion magazine of all time, *Très Chic*. None of those amazing things would have happened if she hadn't started Sew Zoey. It seemed wrong—even worse, totally unfair—that she would lose that because some mystery people were acting mean. If she stopped blogging, she'd also miss the Sew Zoey readers. Even though they hadn't met, they felt like friends.

Zoey knew one thing for sure: No matter what,

even if she stopped blogging, she would never stop sewing, sketching, and coming up with ideas for clothes. That was as much a part of her as breathing.

Marcus came up from the basement, where he'd been practicing his drums since after dinner, and flopped onto the end of the sofa.

"When's Dad coming home?" Zoey asked. "He's hardly been home all week."

She knew she sounded whiny, but . . . she missed having her dad around at dinner every night.

"I know, Zo, but Eastern State has a big championship game coming up the week after next, and some of the big players have injuries. Dad has got to do extra PT sessions with them, so they're ready to play."

"I know. It's just . . ." Zoey hesitated.

"It stinks when he comes home late and tired every night."

"Yeah. That," Zoey said. "At least he's not working tomorrow."

"Zoey," Marcus began. "Is everything okay?"

Zoey thought about telling him everything

about the blog, but when she tried to speak, nothing came out. Finally, she mumbled, "Yeah, I just need to talk to Dad."

Marcus shrugged. "Okay, well, I can think of something that will cheer you up in the meantime," Marcus said. "The latest *Très Chic* came in the mail today."

Marcus definitely knew how to make her feel better. A new issue of *Très Chic* to look through?

Zoey's evening was looking up!

The next morning her dad was home, and not only that, he'd made special pancakes with a secret ingredient Zoey and Marcus had to guess.

"Something citrusy," Marcus said.

"Yes . . . Orange zest?" Zoey guessed.

"You got it!" Mr. Webber said. "And here's some freshly squeezed orange juice from the de-zested oranges."

It was great having him around, and not tired and distracted like he'd been all week.

"What time are we meeting this young lady with the blog?" her dad asked. "And where?"

"Ten thirty," Zoey said. "At A Stitch in Time. Her name's Allie, and she designs handbags and accessories."

"How old is this Allie again?" Mr. Webber asked.

"She's in high school," Zoey said. "Her mom is coming too."

"Maybe I should start a music site," Marcus said. "Zoey gets to meet all these people and be on TV and in magazines because of her blog. I'm so proud of you, sis!"

Zoey was about to say that it wasn't all about meeting cool people—there were some bad parts too. But she decided to wait and speak to her father when they were alone. Would Marcus be proud of her if he knew what people were saying?

She finally got her opportunity to talk to her dad when they were in the car on the way to A Stitch in Time.

"Dad, I need to talk to you about something."

"Go ahead, Zo. Shoot."

"Well . . . it's my blog. It just started this week, but . . . there have been all these horrible comments on it. Really mean stuff. It's been awful. I've tried blocking the users, but then new users come and say the same kinds of things. I don't know who is doing it . . . but I hate it! It's making Sew Zoey not fun anymore."

"Honey—that's terrible! Why didn't you say something to me before now?"

"You haven't been home that much this week," Zoey pointed out. "And when you have been home, you've been really tired. And I didn't know what to say. I was also a little embarrassed, and I thought I could take care of it myself."

"I'm so sorry, Zoey. I got a little behind on reading your blog since work has been crazy. But I thought I was mostly caught up and"—he paused as he came to a realization—"Oh! I guess I usually just read the blog posts, not the comments."

"That's okay, Dad," Zoey said, remembering her blog posts often received dozens of comments— sometimes more than a hundred. "Besides, I think I deleted all the bad ones, so you might have missed them. I just don't know what else to do. Can you please help me make it stop?"

At that, she burst into tears. They were tears of hurt and tears of relief and tears of frustration, and she couldn't stop them from flowing.

"Of course I will, Zo. I'll do everything I can to get to the bottom of this," her father said. "I'm sorry work has been so crazy that I haven't been around as much this week."

He stopped the car at the red light and looked at her, dabbing her eyes with a tissue before rubbing her back.

"Zoey, I want you to remember you and Marcus are always my number-one priority, no matter what else is going on, so if you're upset about something, you can tell me about it no matter how tired I am from work. Do you understand that?"

Zoey nodded. She felt like if she spoke again, she'd let loose another flood of tears. Maybe that wouldn't be such a bad thing.

"Okay, then. I mean it. Anything. Don't forget."

The light changed, and they continued up the street, then turned into the parking lot for A Stitch in Time.

"Leave this to me, Zoey," her dad said as he

pulled into a spot. "I have an idea about what we can do."

Zoey was so relieved that her dad was handling everything now and that he hadn't totally freaked out and told her she couldn't ever blog again. She wished she *had* spoken to him earlier.

They stayed in the parked car for a few minutes. Mr. Webber gave Zoey one of his famous bear hugs, and Zoey felt better than she had in days.

"Just take some deep breaths, and we'll go in when you're ready," he said.

"Do I look okay?" Zoey asked, glancing at her red-rimmed eyes in the mirror on the passenger-side's visor.

"You look beautiful, baby," he said. "Inside and out."

Feeling like a weight had been taken off her shoulders, Zoey had a smile on her face when she walked through the doors of A Stitch in Time. She was immediately greeted with a big smile in return from the owner, Jan.

"Zoey! I hear you've come to meet another of

my favorite customers, Allie," Jan said.

"That's right. We're both going to be in a feature about young designers for the online edition of *Très Chic*," Zoey said.

"I saw it in your blog," Jan said. "So exciting! Allie said they're going to shoot a few pictures in the store." Then she turned to Zoey's dad. "And you must be Mr. Webber."

"I prefer to go by the name Dad of the Designer," Zoey's dad joked. "But Mr. Webber works too."

Jan laughed as she came out from behind the counter.

"Allie and her mom are in the notions aisle. Come on and I'll introduce you."

"Jan, if you don't mind—can I leave Zoey in your capable hands while I make a quick phone call?" Mr. Webber asked. "I'll be back soon."

"It would be my pleasure," Jan said, tucking Zoey's hand in the crook of her elbow and leading her toward the notions.

Allie was looking at decorative trim, one of Zoey's favorite sections, as her mom perused the buttons. Allie was almost as tall as Libby, with really long, really curly brown hair.

"Allie Lovallo, I'd like you to meet Zoey Webber," Jan said. "Two of my favorite young customers."

"Hi, Zoey!" Allie said, her face lighting up with a wide smile. "It's so great to meet you. I love your blog."

"It's nice to meet you, too," Zoey said. "Your bags are amazing."

"How long have you been blogging?" Allie asked.

"Not very long," Zoey said. "One of my friends, Priti, suggested it as a way of showing off my designs. Her mom has a food blog."

"I love the name Sew Zoey."

"One of my other friends, Kate, came up with that. I guess it was kind of a group effort!" Zoey said, smiling as she remembered. It wasn't that long ago, but so much had happened because of it. "How about you?"

"I started a few years ago, because I wanted to show my bags and accessories to people besides my family and friends. I've linked my blog to an Etsy store now, so I'm even starting to sell things. The money will come in handy for college."

"Wow. That's awesome," Zoey said. "College seems so far away to me."

"Before you know it, you'll be a junior like me, and then it'll be right around the corner," Allie said.

"Where are you thinking about going?" Zoey asked.

"My top choice is Parsons The New School for Design," Allie said. "But I'm looking at a whole list of schools."

"Wait. . . . You mean I could go to college to study fashion design?"

Allie laughed. "Sure! That's why I want to go to Parsons. Because when I graduate and get a job, I want to be doing the thing I love doing best in the whole world—designing accessories."

Zoey tried to imagine going to school all day and getting to study fashion design instead of social studies with Mr. Dunn.

"That sounds like heaven," Zoey said wistfully.

"I was thinking—we should do a joint Etsy store, with you designing the outfits and me designing the accessories." Allie said. "What do you think? We could call it 'Fashion from A to Z' or something."

"I love it!" Zoey exclaimed. "Seriously, we should do that. After the *Très Chic* feature comes out."

"Sounds like a plan," Allie declared.

They took a stroll around the store, talking about ideas for projects and pointing out fabrics they loved. Zoey felt pretty comfortable and finally worked up the courage to ask Allie the big question.

"Hey, Allie, I was wondering," started Zoey. "Have you ever had people post really mean stuff on your blog? Like, horrible stuff?"

Allie took a deep breath before speaking. "Yeah, unfortunately," she said. "It was last year. And they also posted on my social networks."

"What did you do?" Zoey asked.

"Well, it wasn't easy, but eventually I told my parents about it," she replied. "You should too."

Zoey nodded. "I just told my dad. But it helps to know it happened to you too, and you're still blogging."

Allie gave Zoey a hug. "It'll all work out. Hang in there."

Before Zoey knew it, her dad was walking down the aisle with Allie's mom, and the parents were telling the girls it was time to go home.

"See you in *Très Chic*!" she called to Allie as they waved good-bye in the parking lot.

"Did you have fun?" her dad asked as they started home.

"Definitely! Did you know I could go to college to study fashion design?" Zoey asked. "How cool would that be?"

"If you are still passionate about sewing and design when you're ready for college, then it would be very cool," Mr. Webber said. "Let's see how you feel closer to the time."

Zoey couldn't imagine wanting to do anything else. But then again, last night she was ready to give up blogging because of what was happening on Sew Zoey.

"You said you had an idea about what to do about my blog. . . . What is it?" she asked.

"Leave it to me, honey. I'll let you know when I sort it out."

Zoey wanted to know more, but just then her

phone buzzed with a text. It was Kate.

Are you home yet? Kate texted.

I'll be back in 10, Zoey thumbed back.

Come over RIGHT AWAY! Your supersleuth friends have discovered a CLUE! read Kate's message.

"Dad, is it okay if I go over to Kate's when we get home?" she asked.

"Sure," her father said. "I have to do some grocery shopping if you kids want to eat next week."

OK, C U soon, Zoey wrote back to Kate.

When they pulled into the driveway, she hesitated before getting out of the car.

"Dad, thanks for not freaking out."

Her father pulled her over for a hug.

"Who says I'm not freaking out?" he said. "Dads tend to do that when people are being mean to their kids." He smiled. "I'm just trying not to show it and focusing on getting to the bottom of this."

"Well, thanks for that," Zoey said, getting out of the car.

It only took a minute to walk down the street to the Mackey house. Kate answered the door, practically buzzing with excitement.

"Come on upstairs!" she said. "Libby and Priti are here—and we've made a breakthrough in the Case of the Cruel Comments!"

Kate bounded up the stairs, taking them two at a time. Zoey followed her, racing to keep up, wondering what her friends had discovered.

Libby and Priti were lounging on Kate's bed, looking at her laptop, but Priti jumped up and gave Zoey a huge hug as soon as she walked into the room.

"Guess what we figured out!" she accidentally shouted into Zoey's ear.

"Um . . . I don't know," Zoey said, rubbing her ear. "If my ears still work after that, maybe you can tell me?"

"Oh, sorry," Priti said. "I guess I got a little carried away. It's nice to have something *good* happen for once."

"Yeah, it's pretty exciting," Libby said. "We've discovered a clue about who's writing the mean stuff on your blog."

Zoey hopped onto the bed next to Libby.

"Okay. So . . . what is it?"

"Well, whoever is writing these comments knows you," Kate said. "In fact, we're pretty sure they go to Mapleton Prep. Or at least one of them does."

Zoey's stomach turned over. She wasn't sure if knowing that made her feel better or worse.

"How do you know?" she asked.

Kate pulled the laptop closer to herself.

"Promise you won't get mad . . . ," she said.

"I promise," Zoey said.

"Well, I took screenshots of some of the nasty comments before you deleted them, because I was thinking of telling Mom about them. I know I said I wouldn't say anything, but I was really worried. And I wanted to save the evidence."

She looked at Zoey, checking to see if she was mad, but when Zoey didn't seem angry, she continued. "When we went back and read through the blog posts they were commenting on, one of them said something that the person could only have known if they'd actually seen you that day."

Kate scrolled through Zoey's blog posts till she got to the one about Twin Day.

"See—you talk about our outfits for Twin Day

in this post, and you mention Priti's outfit is red, but you never say the color of your dress," she said.

"But Sherlock Priti and Libby Watson here, using our astounding powers of deduction, realized one of the comments mentioned that your outfit was *purple!*" Priti said with no small amount of triumph.

"Mainly, the one who said, 'That purple peace outfit looked like something a cat vomited up,'" Libby said. "See, whoever wrote that couldn't have known your dress was purple unless they'd seen you wearing it. Or knew someone who'd seen you wearing it."

"So that's why we figure it's probably someone— or more than one someone—who goes to Mapleton Prep," Kate concluded.

"You guys are the best supersleuth friends a girl could have," Zoey declared. "I can't believe you went to all this trouble."

Her friends all looked at her like she'd grown another head out of her shoulder.

"Well, duh! Why wouldn't we?" Priti asked. "If

someone messes with you, they're messing with all of us."

"Yeah," Kate agreed. "We're a team, and we look after one another."

"We're not going to let anyone make you give up Sew Zoey," Libby said. "No way."

The problems with her blog had really been getting Zoey down, but knowing she'd told her dad and she had the support of her amazing friends made her feel like stopping her blog would only let whomever was behind this win.

"You're right," Zoey said. "I'm not going to stop doing Sew Zoey. No way. Why should I give them the satisfaction?"

"You shouldn't!" Libby agreed.

"I'm so glad we're a team," Zoey said. "And I just had the most amazing idea. Since I couldn't have done any of this without you—without you Sew Zoey wouldn't even exist—I'm going to ask the *Très Chic* editor if you can be in the photo shoot at my house with me."

"Seriously?" Priti asked. "That would be *so cool*."

"Seriously. I'll e-mail her as soon as I get home,"

Zoey promised. "I want our team photo in the feature."

"Wow! My aunt will be so excited that I'm going to be in a fashion magazine," Libby said. Her aunt was a buyer at H. Cashin's department store.

"Um . . . that's really nice of you, Zo, but . . . what do I have to *wear*?" Kate asked. "I mean, this is *Très Chic*. Does that mean we have to be dressed up all glamorous and chichi?"

Zoey laughed. "No! Don't worry. It's a feature about young designers, not haute couture designers. Just be yourself. You could wear those cute red skinny jeans with the white collared shirt. How about that?"

"Okay," Kate said, relieved.

"I almost forgot!" Zoey exclaimed. "You'll probably need your parents to sign release forms for the photos at my house. I'll e-mail them to you tonight."

Libby nodded and Kate said "okay."

"Wait. Both of them?" Priti asked.

"Both parents? Yeah, probably," Zoey replied.

"Why?" Priti continued. "My mom has the flu and, um, can't be in the same room as my dad . . .

or any of us really. Sorry, Zo. . . ."

"I thought your dad had the flu?" Zoey asked without thinking.

Then she caught Kate's and Libby's faces, which looked like a combination of concern and confusion. Was Priti making up the whole thing?

"Right. I guess he gave it to my mom." Priti lowered her eyes and bit her lip. "Whatever."

"Are you okay?" Zoey asked, reaching out to rub Priti's shoulder.

Priti shrugged it off. Then her face softened. "Sorry, guys. You know what, it's no big deal. And I really don't want to talk about it, anyway."

As Zoey walked home later, she thought about how sorry she was that Priti was going through something. Sure, it hadn't been the greatest week Zoey had ever had, but it was over now, and she had her friends and family to thank for getting through it. She was making progress on solving the Case of the Cruel Comments. She had a photo shoot to look forward to, and most of all, she had the best friends and family in the entire universe.

CHAPTER 8

Cut It Out!

Did you see the spread devoted to laser-cut clothing in the latest issue of *Très Chic*? Recently, I've been feeling laser cut to the core. But things are looking up, and at least laser-cut things are totally in style right now. And I'm getting a little help from my friends. You know that saying, "A problem shared is a problem halved"? Well, it's true. I've been trying to deal with the blog problems all by myself, and all it did was make me stressed out during Spirit Week. I finally talked to my dad, and he said he has an idea of how to deal with it and I should leave it to him. Not to be outdone, my friends were super-duper detectives and they've done some sleuthing of their own.

As Kate pointed out earlier, we're all on the same team. And my team is A-W-E-S-O-M-E! They cheer me on, cheer me up, and fight in my corner. And thanks to them, I've decided I'm not going to let a couple of meanies stop me from posting on Sew Zoey. No way! They're the ones who should cut it out. That's the inspiration for today's designs, get it? Cut it out? LOL.

Once I made the decision, I felt so happy about it, I practically danced down the street and back to my house, and as soon as I got home, I ran straight up here, because I had the idea for the cut-it-out–inspired dress and I wanted to get it down on paper. I even cut out a paper doll and designed some cute outfits for her. The fact that I was so fired up, full of creativity and new ideas, was how I knew it was the right decision.

This weekend I got to meet one of the other designers who is going to be featured in the *Très Chic* piece, and she is awesome! Go on over to Always Allie Accessories and check out her bags and things. She has a shop set up and everything. She's a junior in high school, and she's thinking about studying fashion design in college. The thought of being able to go to school and learn about designing and making clothes is like . . . *heaven*! Sign me up! Dad says I have to wait and see if I'm still interested in all of this when it comes time to go to college—but I can't imagine not wanting to sew, ever.

It's a busy week coming up. The *Très Chic* photo shoot is on Wednesday. The best part is they're letting my friends be a part of it too. I can't wait! Now I just have to figure out what to wear! Decisions, decisions. ☺

When the assistant principal came to take Zoey out of class on Tuesday morning because Ms. Austen wanted to see her, Zoey got a sinking feeling. Was she going to be questioned about another horrible prank?

"Am I in trouble?" she asked Mrs. Diaz as they walked through the halls to the main office.

"Not that I'm aware of," she said. "Should you be?"

"No!" Zoey assured her quickly. "I was just wondering why Ms. Austen wanted to see me."

"She'll tell you soon enough," Mrs. Diaz said, refusing to give anything away.

Zoey couldn't help noticing Ms. Austen's beautiful blouse and slim pencil skirt when she walked into her office, or the fact that she topped it—or rather bottomed it—with the most amazing t-strapped shoes. If she was getting in trouble for something, at least she could console herself with the fact that the person reprimanding had really great fashion sense.

"Have a seat, Zoey. I've just had a call from your father," Ms. Austen said.

Uh-oh, Zoey thought. Had her dad faked her out by playing it cool and now was totally overreacting?

"He told me about the problems you've been having with cyberbullying on your blog," Ms. Austen continued.

"Well, yeah. I had a bunch of mean comments on there last week," Zoey said. "It wasn't fun. But is that cyberbullying?"

"Whatever you call it, being bullied is *never* fun," Ms. Austen said firmly. "That's why I take it very seriously. And apparently, Mapleton Prep computers are the source of these comments."

"Wait. Really? How do you know?" Zoey asked.

"Your father said he asked the IT director at Eastern State to help him find the IP addresses of the computers of the people making the comments. He'd initially set your blog to record the IP addresses of all commenters, as a safety measure. He was able to recover the comments you deleted from the trash, and they all originated right here in this school."

"All of them?" Zoey said. "I don't understand. There were so many different usernames. So many people who don't like me or my blog."

"I know that's how it felt," Ms. Austen said. "But it looks like all the comments came from school computers. Whoever did this probably created multiple usernames to make you *think* more people were writing the comments."

"I feel so silly," Zoey said.

"Zoey, listen to me. This is not your fault." She leaned forward. "I promise you I will get to the bottom of this. We have a code of conduct for Internet use, which all students sign at the beginning of the year. Whoever wrote these comments violated the code when they posted from the school computers."

"What will happen to them?" Zoey asked. "They won't get expelled or anything, will they?"

"Well, there certainly will be consequences," Ms. Austen said, "because I want whoever did this to understand that this isn't acceptable behavior for anyone, and especially a Mapleton Prep student."

Zoey had a feeling she knew who might be to blame, but could only tie one of the usernames back to someone who would have seen her at school and disliked her enough to do something like this. Who wrote the other comments? She'd asked the grown-ups for help, and she decided to let them deal with it. She felt a huge weight lift off her shoulders.

"And now for something much more fun," Ms. Austen said, reaching into her drawer and withdrawing a padded envelope. "It seems you've received another package from your fashion fairy godmother, the mysterious Fashionsista."

As far as Zoey was concerned, that definitely *was* a great surprise. Packages from Fashionsista never failed to lift her spirits.

Zoey took the envelope, and Ms. Austen handed her an ivory-handled letter opener that she kept on her desk. When Zoey slit the envelope open, a small box slid out, and a card with an artistic black and white photograph of sticks and stones on the front.

Dear Zoey,
I know you've been having some unpleasantness on Sew Zoey recently. Here's a little gift to remind you that you have friends and supporters, and you most definitely should "stick" with it!
Your friend and fan,
Fashionsista

Zoey opened the box, and inside was a silver bracelet, shaped to look like a string of twigs, studded with round gemstones.

"How lovely!" Ms. Austen said. "I've seen that in the Museum of Modern Art catalog. Fashionsista must think a lot of you to send a gift like that."

Zoey tried to slip the bracelet around her wrist.

"Here, let me help you with the clasp," Ms. Austen said.

When it was fastened, Zoey held out her arm so they could both admire the bracelet. It was thin and delicate, but the way the twigs were linked together gave it an appearance of great strength.

"Your father told me you were thinking of giving up on Sew Zoey because of the nasty comments," Ms. Austen said. "I hope you'll listen to your friend Fashionsista and stick with it."

"Don't worry," Zoey said, glancing down at the bracelet on her wrist. "I will."

The next morning was Wednesday, and even though it was the day of the *Très Chic* shoot, Zoey's excitement was tinged with apprehension.

"Do you think having the reporter and the camera guy there, following me around at school, is going to set off Ivy?" Zoey asked Kate in a low voice as they rode on the bus to school.

"I don't know," Kate answered. "But, Zo, you can't stop doing exciting and awesome things because you're worried it will make Ivy mad. That would just be wrong. You'd be letting her win."

Zoey touched the stick bracelet lightly with her finger.

"You're right," she said. "This *is* exciting and awesome, and I'm going to enjoy it, even if it does put Ivy's nose out of joint."

And when she reported to Ms. Austen's office first thing, so she could meet with the photographer, the makeup artist, and the *Très Chic* writer who would be doing the interview, Zoey really *did* start to have fun.

"Oh my gosh," she said, looking at the makeup artist's kit of rainbow-colored lipsticks, eyeshadows, blushes, and more. "Is this really happening? I feel like a princess!"

"It is happening! My name is Sophie, by the

way," the woman replied. "Everyone loves the lipstick palettes, but today I'm just going to give you some very light, natural touch-ups."

Zoey closed her eyes as the woman applied shimmery eyeshadow to her eyelids. The whole thing felt like a dream—a wonderful dream!

When it was okay to open her eyes again, she watched in the mirror as Sophie added a rosy blush, translucent powder, and then brushed and sprayed her hair to make sure there were "no pesky flyaways to distract the eye."

Then Sophie grabbed a tube of lip gloss and started to unscrew the top when Zoey stopped her.

"Hold on!" Zoey said, reaching into her bag and grabbing the lip gloss Fashionsista, her fashion fairy godmother, had given to her for her *Fashion Showdown* appearance. "Can I use this instead? It's for good luck!"

"Sure!" said Sophie. She dabbed a little on Zoey's lips. "There. I think you're ready!"

They ventured out into the hallway to take some shots of Zoey taking books out of her locker. A few students played it cool and walked by, as if seeing a fashion shoot in the school hallway was something they saw every day. But most of them stared curiously, and a few milled around, obviously hoping that they might be caught in the background of the shot and get their own small chance of fame.

Finally, Phil, the photographer, got frustrated.

"Listen, kids, if you want to be in the background, you can't just stand there, gawking at the camera," he said. "Try to look natural, like you're passing through the hall on your way to your next class or getting something from your locker, just as you would if I wasn't here."

From the corner of her eye, Zoey noticed Ivy, Shannon, and Bree in the group of gawkers, but she tried to not let them spoil her enjoyment of being a star for a day. She was having too much fun answering the reporter's questions and posing for the photographer.

After school, Zoey's dad picked her up—along with Libby, Priti, and Kate—and drove them back to the Webber house for the Team Zoey photo shoot. The

Très Chic team met them there. Sophie worked on Libby, Priti, and Kate while Zoey showed Phil where she worked and blogged, so he could figure out the best setup for the shoot. He even asked Zoey to bring her sewing machine up to her room instead of leaving it on the dining table, since her room was a more unique setting. When they came back downstairs, Zoey saw that even Marcus and her dad were getting some light powder and blush, in case they were in the pictures.

"Don't tell any of the guys on the football team," Mr. Webber said. "I'll never hear the end of it."

"It's nothing to be afraid of," Sophie said. "Makeup is just a tool."

"Yeah, Dad. It's no big deal," Zoey said. "Everyone on TV wears powder. Even sportscasters."

Her dad smiled. "I stand corrected," he said.

"You mean you *sit* corrected," Marcus pointed out.

Zoey bowed her head. She loved her family, but they could be *so* embarrassing. Did they have to show the *Très Chic* people what kind of corny jokes they made in the Webber household? Then she remembered she was often the corniest, cheesiest of them all.

"Why don't we go upstairs, and you can tell me how your friends inspired you to start Sew Zoey?" the reporter said. "Our editor, Izzy, told us it was a great story."

"And Zoey can introduce you to Marie Antoinette!" Libby said.

"Marie Antoinette?" the writer asked.

"She's my dress form. I called her that because she . . . um . . . doesn't have a head," Zoey said, worrying that the reporter might think she was kind of ghoulish.

But the entire *Très Chic* team burst out laughing.

"Marie Antoinette!" Phil exclaimed. "I love it! We definitely have to get her in some of the pictures. But before we begin, I'm going to need your release forms."

They already had Zoey's form. Libby and Kate handed theirs over quickly.

Priti studied her release form, but didn't pass it to Phil. Zoey thought she saw Priti shake her head slightly.

"What's the matter?" asked Phil. "Did you forget to get it signed?"

"No," Priti said. "Here, take it."

Zoey could see that one of the signatures was smudged, and an edge of the paper was torn.

"Great!" said Phil, sticking them into his bag. "Four release forms means it's photo time!"

They moved up to Zoey's room, and the photographer staged the girls, moving Marie Antoinette so she'd be visible in the background.

"Do you have a project you're working on at the moment?" the writer asked.

"Yes," Zoey said, taking out a minidress she'd been experimenting with after watching a movie from the 1960s with her dad and Marcus. Phil had Zoey pose with needle and thread as Priti held scissors; Libby, a tape measure; and Kate, some trim. It seemed really fake and unnatural to Zoey, but she knew they were the professionals.

"Okay, Priti, can you smile for me now?" the photographer asked. He snapped a whole bunch of pictures and then stopped. "Let's change the pose slightly, but it would really help if I could get you to smile, Priti. Everyone else in the picture is smiling like the Cheshire cat, but you look like your puppy just died."

"I'm sorry," Priti said, sounding very subdued. "I promise I'll smile this time."

Zoey couldn't understand what was wrong with her friend. It was so unlike her. Usually, Priti would be in her element doing this kind of thing. She normally loved having her picture taken and was the most smiley and bubbly of all of them.

This time, Phil wanted Zoey posed with her fingers on her laptop, as if she were in the middle of writing a new blog post, and the girls huddled around her, leaning in to look at the screen, pretending to be excited by her fabulous new design.

"Can we be on the bed instead of by my worktable?" Zoey asked. "That's where I normally blog."

"Let's try it both ways," the photographer proposed.

He kept having to remind Priti to smile after every shot. Zoey had been worried something was going on with Priti for a while. Now she was absolutely 100 percent sure something was wrong.

Before they left the bedroom, Phil wanted a fun shot of them giving Marie Antoinette a group hug.

"I don't know if we'll use it in the feature, but let's take it, anyway, just for giggles," he said.

"Can you send it to us?" Zoey asked.

"Sure," the photographer said. "If it's not used in the feature, I'll make sure the editor forwards it to you."

After taking some family pictures with Marcus and her dad in the kitchen, pretending to make and eat dinner, the *Très Chic* team packed up their gear.

There sure is a lot of pretending *in these photo shoots,* Zoey thought.

"We've got everything we need," the reporter said. "Our editor will e-mail you the link as soon as the feature is live. Good luck with your designs!"

"Thanks," Zoey said as the crew waved good-bye and left the room. "I still feel like I'm going to wake up in a minute and find out this was all a dream! But it wasn't, was it? It's been so much fun!"

"It has," Libby agreed. "I can't wait to see the pictures."

"Me too," Kate said. "Especially the ones with us all hugging Marie Antoinette."

Kate walked home, and Libby's mom came to pick her up, but as had so often been the case recently, Priti seemed in no rush to go home.

"Priti, what's the matter?" Zoey asked. "The photographer had to fight to get a smile out of you during the shoot, which isn't like you at all. To tell you the truth, you haven't been yourself for a few weeks now."

Priti fidgeted with the rubber bracelets she was wearing, twisting them around her wrist, but she didn't say anything.

"Come on. I know something is wrong, Priti. Don't you want to talk about it?"

When Priti looked up at Zoey, her brown eyes were brimming with tears. "It's my parents, Zo. They're . . . having problems. They've been fighting like crazy. You heard them that day when we practiced at my house, right?"

Zoey nodded.

"It's been like that for a while. They won't agree on anything anymore. You have no idea how hard it was to get them to sign the release form for the photo shoot. Everything is an argument, even good things. My mom signed it, but my dad thought it wasn't a good idea for me to be in a magazine. Finally, he caved when I started crying."

"Gosh, I'm sorry," Zoey said, now understanding why Priti's release form was in such bad shape.

"You know, I've been trying to ignore it, because talking about it makes it feel . . . real," Priti confessed, wiping away a tear. Her hand was shaking, so Zoey held it in hers. "But I can't ignore it, no matter how hard I try. It is real. Last night they sat us all down and said they're starting couples counseling, which means they are going to get divorced, doesn't it? And if they get divorced then what will happen? We'll probably have to move, and then I wouldn't be able to go to Mapleton Prep, and then I'll miss my friends and—"

Priti couldn't hold it in any longer. She burst into tears.

Zoey rubbed Priti's back to comfort her. When Priti's sobs had slowed down, Zoey got her some tissues.

"Have you tried talking to Sashi and Tara?" she asked.

"Y-yes." Priti sniffed. "But they just snap at me to stop talking about it, because they're worried about it too, and they have even more to worry about with getting into college and stuff."

"I'm not an expert or anything, but . . . if your parents are doing counseling, doesn't that mean they're trying to work things out so they can stay together?" Zoey asked.

"I guess," Priti said. "But . . . what if it doesn't work? What if they *do* get d-divorced? It's going to be terrible."

Another tear escaped from her eye, and she blotted it away with a tissue.

"It would stink if they get divorced," Zoey agreed. "I can't say it wouldn't. But your parents will still love you no matter what happens between them."

"I g-guess."

"And we'll all be here to support you, come what may. BFFs, remember?"

"I know, but . . . it's divorce, Zo. The D word. Things would never be the same," Priti said.

"But that doesn't mean you wouldn't ever be happy," Zoey pointed out. "I mean, Aunt Lulu got divorced, and she seems happy enough."

"Aunt Lulu was married?" Priti asked, surprised. She'd always thought of Zoey's aunt as single.

"Uh-huh. It wasn't for very long, only a few years. And they never had kids, obviously."

Zoey got up from the bed and stretched.

"The point is, she got divorced, but she's okay. And no matter what happens, you'll be okay."

Priti heaved a big shuddering sigh.

"I know you're right, but I can't seem to stop worrying about all the what-ifs? It's like my brain has short-circuited and it's stuck on worry mode."

"It's not the same, I know, but sometimes when I get superanxious about a big sewing project, it helps me to think about one stitch at a time instead of looking at the whole project and feeling, like, *Help, I'll never be able to do this!*" Zoey said. "So . . . maybe you can just try to think about one day at a time and not worry so much about what might happen—or might not happen? I know it's easier to say and harder to do, but . . ."

"I'll try," Priti said. "Anything has got to be better than being stuck in worry mode."

Zoey had an idea. "I've got the perfect thing to get you unstuck. Come on, let's go downstairs!"

In the kitchen, she got out two bowls, some ice cream, chocolate syrup, and whipped cream.

"Ice-cream-sundae time!" she said. "And then we can watch the latest episode of *Fashion Showdown*. It's on the DVR."

As they settled onto the sofa with their sundaes, Priti smiled a happier, more genuine smile than Zoey had seen on her face all day.

"I feel better already," she said. "Thanks, Zo. For listening. And the sundae. And everything."

"No problem," Zoey said. "That's what BFFs are for."

CHAPTER 9

One Stitch at a Time

I'm so glad I decided to stick with Sew Zoey, because you (other than the nasty commenters who will not be mentioned from now on) have been so amazing and supportive. I want to give a special shout-out and SUPERBIG thank-you to Fashionsista for the beautiful "stick with it" bracelet. I wore it for the *Très Chic* photo shoot, and it reminded me not to let my worry about how people might think or react get in the way of enjoying the fun things that were happening—like being star for a day and being followed around at school by a writer and photographer and makeup artist! I can't wait to see how it turns out.

I'm trying to remember that sometimes when a problem seems too big, it helps to look at it in smaller pieces. Like when you're working on a sewing project and you think you'll never be able to finish it, just think about doing one stitch at a time, and before you know it, the project is a quarter done, then half done, then three-quarters done, and then one day, the thing you thought you'd never be able to complete is *done*, and it looks amazing! This idea inspired the sketches for today's blog.

I'm going to work on taking things one day at a time—one stitch at a time—instead of letting everything and everyone get me down. Things are looking brighter already!

Zoey was happy to see Priti a bit more like her usual self after their talk. At Zoey's suggestion, she ended up confiding in Libby and Kate about the problems at home too, so they all could give her extra TLC when she needed it.

"My parents said they don't *want* to get divorced," Priti told them at lunch. "So I'm hoping everything is going to be okay, and I'm just taking it one stitch at a time, like Zoey says."

"Can I have one of your fries at a time?" Kate asked.

"Me too!" Zoey said. "They smell amazing!"

Priti laughed and passed her fries around for her friends to share.

Early the following week, Zoey got an e-mail from the editor at *Très Chic* telling her the online feature, "A Day in the Life: Ten Teen Designers to Watch" was live on the magazine's website. Hardly able to click on the link because of her excitement, Zoey scrolled through the slideshow of the other designers, reading about how they spent their days at school, their design work, and their dreams for the future. Allie looked great in her photos, and it was fun to see the pictures of her with Jan at A Stitch in Time. Allie even mentioned in her interview that Zoey shopped there too! Zoey sent her an e-mail, thanking her and reminding her they should do a "Fashion from A to Z" Etsy store together.

Her own spread was awesome. There was a picture of her and Ms. Austen standing by Zoey's locker, with a crowd of students milling around, trying to look like nothing special was happening. If Zoey looked really carefully, she could see Ivy, Shannon, and Bree in the corner of the frame, but their faces were blurry, because the focus was on Zoey. She wondered if Ivy would be happy she was in the picture or mad because she was blurry. Whatever. Zoey wasn't going to let it bother her.

Zoey's favorite picture was of all the girls hugging Marie Antoinette. She was glad the editor did use the "fun shot," and she decided to write to the photographer and ask for copies for her friends. She had a great idea for decorating cute picture frames to put them in!

The best part of all, Zoey thought, was that she

was in such great company and that a magazine like *Très Chic* considered her a *real designer*. When she went to school the next day, she felt like she didn't need the "sticks and stones" bracelet to remind her not to let Ivy get her down—but she wore it anyway, because she liked it so much.

People kept coming up to her in the hall and saying things like, "Hey, I saw you on the *Très Chic* website!" and "Cool feature in *Très Chic*!" Even Lorenzo had seen it, and Zoey was pretty sure that fashion magazines weren't his usual reading fare.

"My mom reads *Très Chic*. She showed me the pictures of you guys," he said when she walked into English. "Totally awesome!"

"Really? Thanks!" Zoey said, hoping she wasn't starting to blush the way she always seemed to when Lorenzo spoke to her.

If looks could kill, the one Ivy gave her just then would have done Zoey some serious damage.

"Did you see me in the picture?" Ivy asked Lorenzo.

"Uh, no," Lorenzo said. "Were you in it?"

Zoey sat in her chair before Ivy could give her

another death glare. If it was really Ivy behind the nasty comments, she had a feeling she'd be in for more tonight when she got home.

"That was a really cool feature about you," Gabe said, swiveling around in his chair to smile at her.

"*You* read *Très Chic*?" Zoey asked, amazed.

"Well, not *usually*." Gabe smiled again. "I'm normally more a *Sports Illustrated* or *Scientific American* kind of guy. But when one of your friends is one of Ten Teen Designers to Watch, a guy has to make sacrifices."

"Thanks for your sacrifice," Zoey said. "I hope it wasn't too painful."

"It was actually pretty cool. I never knew you had a headless dummy called Marie Antoinette. Do you ever wake up in the middle of the night and think that you're in the middle of a zombie apocalypse when you see her shadow?"

Zoey laughed.

"She's a dress form, not a dummy, and no. Marie Antoinette is *waaaaay* too well dressed to be a zombie."

"Who says zombies can't be well dressed? If the apocalypse hit the fashion district, there could totally be well-dressed zombies."

"You think about the strangest things," Zoey said. "Funny, but strange."

Still, for the rest of class, she was sketching zombie fashions in the margins of her note-book. She showed them to Gabe at the end of the period.

"See!" he said, grinning. "I knew you'd get it!"

"Thanks for the idea," Zoey said. "I can use it for a Z design when Allie and I do our 'Fashion from A to Z' project."

"Who'd have thought you'd be getting fashion ideas from Gabe Monaco?" Priti said when Zoey showed them the zombie fashion sketches at lunch. "I mean, it's not like he's a bad dresser, but . . ."

"I get my ideas everywhere," Zoey said. "That's the exciting thing about them. I never know where I'm going to find the next one."

"I know! Remember when you got the idea for that cool dress at the Eastern State Game?" Kate said. "I was too busy watching them play to think about anything else."

Zoey definitely remembered that dress. The day she wore it to school was the first time Lorenzo paid attention to her.

"Have you checked the traffic on your blog lately?" Libby said. "I mean, if *Gabe and Lorenzo* are reading the *Très Chic* thing, I bet Sew Zoey must have lots of new readers."

Zoey hadn't even thought to check last night after she got the *Très Chic* link.

"I don't know," she said. "But now I can't wait to go home after school and check!"

Sure enough, Sew Zoey was showing major traffic. There were a bunch of comments from names Zoey didn't recognize, telling her they'd found out about her blog from reading about her in *Très Chic* and complimenting her on her designs. She scanned down the comments—there were more than a hundred! Many were from her regular readers, saying how awesome it was that more people were discovering Sew Zoey.

Then Zoey saw something she couldn't believe. She rubbed her eyes and blinked a few times to make sure she was seeing properly. Because there, on her blog, was a comment from DaphneShawNY, the designer who Zoey looked up to as one of her biggest inspirations!

Hi, Zoey! I'm a big fan of your blog—usually a lurker, but I read the posts and the comments. I'm sorry you've had to deal with such unpleasantness recently. Every creative person has to learn to deal with critics because every art form is subjective. But when you're in the public eye, some of them can be pretty nasty, and sometimes, it's because they're jealous of your talent and your success. You have to learn to develop a thick skin, hold your head up high, and be proud of your fabulous self. Remember that saying about how "sticks and stones will break my bones, but words will never hurt me"? Well, words DO hurt sometimes. Even so, try not to let them get to you. You're a star. Keep up the great work!

Daphne

Zoey fingered the bracelet she was wearing on her wrist. It seemed like everyone was talking about the sticks-and-stones thing lately.

She read through the post again, still hardly able to believe that Daphne Shaw read her blog and looked at her designs and *liked* them.

A few comments down there was *another* one from DaphneShawNY:

> I forgot to mention: The next time you're in New York, do let me know, so I can give you a personal tour of my studio.
> Daphne.

Zoey shrieked with excitement, jumped out of her chair, and ran to her brother's room.

"Marcus! How soon will Dad be home?"

"Why? What's the matter?"

"Nothing's the matter! Everything's AMAZING!" Zoey said, leaping onto his bed and bouncing up and down.

"Ooookay. . . . Can I ask what news has got you bouncing on my bed?"

"You'll never believe it," Zoey said.

"Try me."

"Guess who commented on my blog!"

Marcus screwed up his face as if he were thinking really hard.

"Um . . . Justin Bieber?"

"No, better than that! DAPHNE SHAW!"

"OMG!" Marcus shrieked in a high-pitched falsetto, like he was really excited. "Wait, who is Daphne Shaw again?"

Zoey took the pillow from the bed and threw it at him.

"You know! Only my favorite designer ever!"

"Ooh! *That* Daphne Shaw. That's awesome, Zo. What did she say?"

"That she's been reading my blog for a while and she's sorry I've had to deal with all the nasty comments, but I have to get used to criticism if I'm going to be a famous designer and stuff, but the best part is . . . SHE INVITED ME FOR A PERSONAL TOUR OF HER STUDIO WHEN I'M IN NEW YORK!"

"Wow!" Marcus wasn't pretending to be excited now. "That's really amazing, Zoey. I'm sure she also said you should bring your bestest brother in the whole world with you on this trip to New York. "

"I think she forgot to add that part." Zoey grinned. "Maybe if he's super-duper nice to me."

"He's *always* super-duper nice to you, isn't he?" Marcus said.

"So when is Dad getting home?"

Marcus glanced at the clock.

"He should be home in about half an hour."

Zoey tried to do her homework, but it was too hard to concentrate while she was waiting for her father to come home. Anyway, she *had* to call all her friends to tell them about the post from Daphne Shaw.

As soon as she heard her dad's car pull into the driveway and the garage door open, Zoey raced down the stairs. She was waiting for him in the kitchen before he even walked into the house.

"DAD! You'll never guess what happened!"

"What ever happened to, 'Hi, Dad, how was your day?'" Dad asked.

"Hi, Dad, how was your day? GUESS WHAT HAPPENED?" Zoey said.

Her father put down his bag, poured himself a glass of juice, and sat down at the kitchen table. "Well, how about you tell me, since it's been a long day at work?" he said. "Good news?"

"Daphne Shaw, who is only my favorite designer ever and my biggest inspiration, COMMENTED ON MY BLOG!" Zoey said. "She said she reads it all the time. But best of all—she invited me for a personal tour when I'm in New York. So, Dad—we have to book a trip to New York right away, so we can go visit her studio!"

"Honey, we're not going to do that tonight—"

"But DAD! It's Daphne Shaw! What if she changes her mind?"

"Zoey, Daphne Shaw is a public figure. She wouldn't have made an offer like that on a public blog if she didn't mean it."

"But—"

"And you have school and I have work. It was one thing to take a day off for *Fashion Showdown*, but school is important."

"I know," Zoey said, but she felt like a deflated balloon.

Her dad noticed her subdued expression.

"You know another thing, Zo—you'd want to give Ms. Shaw some notice. She might want to plan something special. I don't think showing up on her doorstep tomorrow is a great idea."

In her excitement, Zoey hadn't thought of that. "Oh. I see what you mean."

"Don't worry, honey," Mr. Webber said. "We'll plan a trip to New York when the time is right, and we'll make sure that when we do, you get to visit Daphne Shaw and tour her studio. Dad's promise."

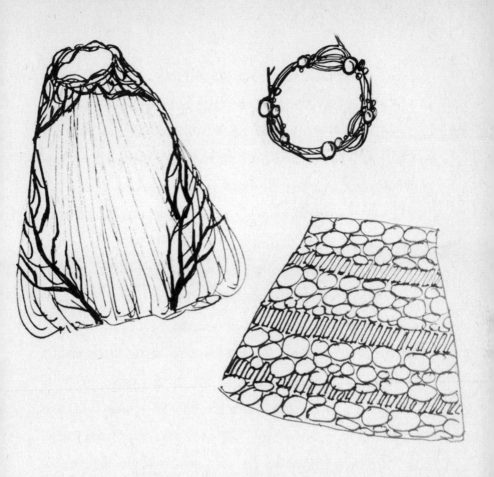

CHAPTER 10

Sticks and Stones

Welcome to all the new readers who have come to Sew Zoey from reading about me and my blog in the Day in the Life of a Designer feature on the *Très Chic* website. I hope you stay and comment on my designs, because I've learned so much from my regular readers.

Just, when you make a critique, think about how you would feel if someone were making it about something you created. It's great to be honest—the only way I'll get better is if people give me real feedback about the stuff I make—but you don't have to be mean-spirited.

Today's sketches are inspired by one of my readers—someone I didn't even know read my blog until yesterday, but who's been my inspiration since before I even started it—Daphne Shaw! Thank you, Ms. Shaw, for leaving such an encouraging comment and such great advice. I'll do my best to remember about "sticks and stones." Most of all, thank you, THANK YOU, Ms. Shaw, for the invitation to visit your studio the next time I'm in New York. I wish it could be tomorrow, but Dad says I have to go to school. Anyway, I hope it's sometime very, very soon. It's given me something superspecial to look forward to!

One thing I've realized is how designing clothes—I guess like doing anything creative—is really personal. So it hurts a lot when people don't like your work and it feels really great when they do. I guess that's what Ms. Shaw means about having to develop a thick skin if you're going to be a professional—learning to not let it hurt so much when people don't like your work. Because the fact is, not everyone likes the same things, and, really, that's a good thing, because if they did, it would be really boring—we'd all be wearing the same clothes. It would be just like when we had to wear a uniform at our school. It's a lot more fun now that everyone can choose what to wear every day. Okay, so sometimes there are people who don't like what I wear, and they tell me. And sometimes they aren't very nice about it. But as long as I feel like I did my best, I'm going to try to let it roll off my well-dressed shoulders!

Before she went to school the next day, Zoey checked her blog to see if any more comments had come in from the *Très Chic* feature. At the bottom of more than one hundred and fifty comments, there was one that had come in after she had checked last night.

I don't know what makes Zoey think she's so special. She looks like she got her clothes at a thrift store.

She deleted it and blocked the user. It made her wonder what was going on with the investigation at Mapleton Prep. Would the IT director be able to find out who had posted the comments, and if so, what would Ms. Austen do?

That's when Zoey realized she was late. She logged off and ran to catch the bus.

She was in social studies when the person sitting behind her tapped her on the back and passed her a note. Zoey waited to open it until Mr. Dunn turned to face the Smart Board.

Curiously, the note was from Shannon, asking Zoey to meet her by the vending machine before the next class.

Zoey wondered why Shannon would want to talk to her. Or was it part of a prank? Was Shannon getting her to the vending machine so Ivy and Bree could play a trick on her?

There was a time when Zoey and Shannon used to pass notes back and forth to each other all the time. Back in elementary school, when they were friends. Before Shannon started hanging out with

Ivy. Zoey decided to give Shannon the benefit of the doubt. She scribbled "Okay" and surreptitiously passed the note back.

The rest of the period seemed to drag by. It was harder than usual to pay attention to Mr. Dunn when Zoey kept thinking about all the possibilities of what Shannon might want to say to her. When the bell finally rang, she almost jumped out of her seat.

She left the classroom before Shannon and walked to their rendezvous spot at the vending machine. Shannon skulked up a minute later, checking over her shoulder and pulling Zoey into the alcove by the side of the machine so they were less visible.

"Thanks for coming," Shannon said. She seemed really jumpy and nervous.

"That's okay," Zoey said. "Uh . . . what did you want to meet about?"

"I just . . ." Shannon twisted the hem of the sweater she was wearing in her fist. "I wanted to say that the powder thing—you know, putting it in your hat? Ivy made Bree do it. She said she wouldn't be friends with her otherwise. And she made us post the mean comments on your blog, too. Because of what you said about her snakeskin-patterned dress on *Fashion Showdown*."

"Wait . . . what? I don't understand. I didn't say anything about Ivy or her dress on *Fashion Showdown*."

"Yes, you did," Shannon said. "You saw the dress Ivy wore to the dance, and then there was a dress that was almost identical on *Fashion Showdown*, and you said you didn't like it."

"But . . . the whole segment was taped before I even got to the dance," Zoey said. "How was I supposed to know what dress Ivy was going to wear? I just gave my honest opinion, like I was supposed to do as a judge."

"Oh . . . wow. I didn't know the whole thing was already taped before the dance. It didn't air until later!" Shannon said. "I guess Ivy got it wrong, huh?"

"Yeah, she did." Zoey said, hardly believing her ears.

"But, anyway, you told on us to Ms. Austen

about the hat prank," Shannon said. "We all got in trouble right after you and Libby were in her office."

"I didn't!" Zoey said. "She asked me if I thought you did it, and I said I didn't know who did it. It's not my fault if she thought it was you guys."

Shannon was confused. She'd come prepared to be angry at Zoey for a whole list of things it turned out Zoey hadn't done.

"Well, even if you didn't snitch on us then, we're in serious trouble now," she said. "Mr. Arenzini in the computer lab looked at the logs and figured out Ivy, Bree, and me were the ones on the school computers at the times the comments from the Mapleton Prep IP address were posted on your blog. Ms. Austen called our parents in for a big meeting yesterday, and now we're all on probation because we broke the code of conduct."

"I'm really sorry you're in trouble, Shannon," Zoey said. "But those comments really hurt. They made me feel really bad—so bad I was even thinking of giving up my blog."

Shannon's face turned red. "I'm sorry, Zoey. I really am," Shannon said. "Posting those things was wrong. I shouldn't have listened to Ivy."

"I guess Ivy can be kind of hard to stand up to," Zoey said.

"Yeah," Shannon said. "But don't give up Sew Zoey. I lied when I said the mean things about it. I love reading your blog. I think it's really great."

It wasn't awesome knowing Shannon was one of the people who'd written some of those nasty comments. But hearing she actually loved Sew Zoey made Zoey feel pretty good. After all, there was a time when she and Shannon had been good friends. She didn't want to think of her as an enemy, not really.

But already, Shannon was getting edgy, glancing around, worried Ivy might be nearby and spot her talking to Zoey.

"I better get to class," she said.

"Yeah, me too. But thanks for telling me this," Zoey said before they went their separate ways again.

That weekend, Zoey invited her friends over for a sleepover. Since the one last mean comment the day Daphne Shaw posted on her blog, there hadn't been a single nasty remark on Sew Zoey. It was a relief for her to not be scared to look at her blog every day, and she was beginning to enjoy it again without any worry or hesitation. In fact, she loved the great feedback she was getting from all her new readers.

Marcus and his band were downstairs in the basement practicing while the girls made cookies in the kitchen.

"There's a new episode of *Fashion Showdown* on tonight," Zoey said. "And guess who is one of the judges? Daphne Shaw!"

"You mean your new BFF?" Priti said. "Do you think she'd let me come visit her studio too? I wonder if she gives out free samples?"

"I don't know," Zoey said. "I just hope it's not too long before I can go take her up on her offer."

"I just can't believe Ivy thought you purposely criticized that dress on *Fashion Showdown* because you saw her wearing one like it at the dance," Kate said. "Why would you do that?"

"Maybe because she says mean things about

Zoey, she thinks Zoey would do the same thing?" Libby suggested.

"Or maybe it's like Daphne says—maybe she's jealous or something," Zoey said.

"Well, I'm just glad you don't have to worry about her and Bree and Shannon being nasty on your blog anymore," Priti said. "It would have been awful if you'd had to give up Sew Zoey."

"Hey, something smells good!" Marcus emerged from the basement, followed by the rest of his band-mates. "Any cookies to spare for hungry musicians?"

Zoey checked the timer.

"They come out of the oven in twenty-nine seconds. But if you want some, you have to play our karaoke song for us."

Marcus glanced at his friends. They all nodded except for Dan, the guitar player, who had a pained expression on his face.

Dan finally spoke. "As much as it pains me to play that Top 40 commercial stuff, my stomach is telling me to sell my artistic soul for a cookie."

Marcus looked back at Zoey. "You got yourself a deal, sister."

They all counted down to the oven buzzer. "Five . . . four . . . three . . . two . . . ONE!"

Zoey took out the cookies from the oven, and as soon as they were cool enough to touch, everyone pounced. Within a minute, the tray was empty.

"Those were amazing," said Dan. "They almost make it worth suffering through that song."

"That song is awesome!" Priti exclaimed.

"Yeah, if you're a middle school girl," Dan retorted.

"A deal's a deal," Zoey said. "Come on! Karaoke time!"

They headed down to the basement, and Marcus led off.

Without the entire school watching, Zoey was completely relaxed, and she and her friends had a blast singing and dancing.

"I hate to admit it, but that song is beginning to grow on me," Marcus said.

"Traitor!" Dan exclaimed.

"Play it again!" Priti begged.

Dan groaned, but he went along with it as soon as the rest of the band started playing.

"No more!" he said after the encore. "Twice is my max!"

"It's okay," Zoey said. "*Fashion Showdown* starts soon."

The girls trooped upstairs to the living room and settled in to watch *Fashion Showdown*.

It had been a difficult few weeks, Zoey thought. But Priti seemed a little happier lately, and things were back to normal—in fact, better than ever—on Sew Zoey. It was true. Everything did work out in the end—as long as you took it one stitch at a time.

Who is cute as a button?
Find out in the
next book in
the Sew Zoey series:

CUTE
as a
BUTTON

It's Nifty to be Thrifty

Designing and making clothes is definitely my favorite thing to do, but there's one big catch—buying fabric starts to add up. It's not just the fabric—it's all the trimming, buttons, zippers, sequins, you name it! The only reason I've been able to make so many outfits lately is because of the money I won in the Avalon Fabrics Break-out Designer Contest—and because both Jan at A Stitch in Time and my Aunt Lulu are so great about giving me scrap material. But I'm going from riches to rags, even though I've been doing my best to shop on a budget. My allowance only goes so far and I'm too young to babysit, so Dad said I can do odd jobs around the house to earn money, but there are only so many of those. Lately, he's been paying me to dust the house plants and sew buttons on his shirts! What's an aspiring fashion designer bursting with ideas to do? I've been digging around at the thrift store again, trying to find clothes I can take apart for the fabric. But I loved this dress too much to take it apart. Instead I got creative and "Zoey-fied" it. I made some tweaks here and there and added a belt that used to be my Mom's. Cool, huh?

"Are you sure you don't mind?" Aunt Lulu said for the third time as she stood by the door to leave.

"Mind? We love having Draper here," Zoey said, her arms wrapped around her doggy cousin's neck.

Aunt Lulu's fourteen year-old mutt thumped his tail against the kitchen floor in agreement.

"See? Draper loves being here, too," Zoey said.

"I know he does," Aunt Lulu said, smiling. "And I know you and Marcus will give him lots of love while I'm away at the interior design conference."

"Oh, you can count on that," Marcus said. "Draper will get plenty of love—and treats."

"Not too many treats," Aunt Lulu warned. "He's already overweight."

"He is not," Zoey said. "You are the handsomest dog ever."

Draper licked Zoey's face.

"I'll see you in a few days," Aunt Lulu said, blowing kisses as she walked out the door.

Draper trotted over and let out a soft whine.

"Aw, he misses Aunt Lulu already," Marcus said. "Give him a treat."

Draper's ears pricked up at the word "treat". Zoey wanted to follow Aunt Lulu's advice for at least a few minutes after she left, but Draper seemed so very sad. Just one treat wouldn't hurt.

"Come on, Draper. Treat!" she said, walking over to the tin of treats.

Draper moseyed over to Zoey expectantly.

"Sit," Zoey said.

Draper stood, staring up with his brown eyes.

"Come on, Draper, sit!" she said again.

With a deep sigh and an *If I really must* look, Draper sank onto his rear haunches.

"Good boy, good sit," Zoey crooned, giving him his treat.

"I wonder if Draper ever thinks, *Why do they make me do this just to get a treat?*" Marcus said.

"I think he just cares about getting the treat!"

"You underestimate him," Marcus said.

"No, I don't. I just think he has his priorities straight. If I could get ice cream whenever someone said 'sit' I would totally sit down on command! But now it's time to sit and *sew*, right Draper?"

Draper lumbered up the stairs behind Zoey and

followed her into her room. After a brief, unsuccessful search for hidden treats, he sat under the cute vintage sewing machine table Zoey's dad had bought her so she could work in her bedroom.

The week before, Zoey had seen a dress that she adored in her favorite fashion magazine, *Très Chic*. She wanted it so badly—until she saw the price. But it was *so cute!* That's when she had the idea to make it herself. With Draper's nose resting on her foot, Zoey sketched out ideas for how to copy the dress.

It was comforting to have Draper with her while she worked. He seemed to sense when she was getting frustrated, and he'd give her foot a gentle lick as if to say *Don't worry, Zoey, you'll figure it out*.

Zoey put down her pencil and ducked her head under the table to look at Draper. He lifted his nose and his tail wagged, thumping a steady beat against the carpet.

"You're such a good boy, Draper," Zoey said.

And then she had a fabulous idea. . . .